Shadow in the Dreamlands

The Chronicles of Randy Carter Book 3

Sonya Lawson

SauceBox Press

Contents

Note to Reader (CW)

This book contains scenes that may depict, mention, or discuss abduction, assault, attempted murder, death, decapitation, kidnapping, murder, the occult, and violence. Please take care of yourself as you read.

To all the other inclusive horror nerds out there who
wanted to change the story.

ONE

MANY BAKERS, HOME AND pro, have feared choux pastry. I'd never understood why. People talked about it like it was so complex. For me, it had never been complex. Mix the dough, cook it a bit in a pan, pipe it out, and voilà. There was puffy, light, golden goodness, ready to make éclairs or cream puffs or any number of yummy treats from the seemingly simple dough.

My attitude toward choux had changed one disastrous day. Choux pastry was not forgiving. Make one tiny error in mixing, cooking, piping—anything really—and it went out the window. I'd never known this because I'd somehow made it well from the jump. When I hadn't made it well, I'd discovered something: natural ability could fail, and all there was to fall back on was what I'd learned along the way. All too often, when things seemed easy, the learning stopped. People tended to get cocky, think they had it all down. It was a big mistake a lot of people make in things like baking—a mistake I'd made with choux, my magic, and a whole host of other real important shit in my life.

THE WITCH HOUSE HAD gone down a week before the Carter parents invaded Columbus, which was great. Mom and Dad had fun. They met both Harley and Gareth in person, and I reassured them I was alive and doing well. They assumed I was also seriously dating Gareth, as Merry and Harley were tight. Especially when they found out Harley and Gareth were both introduced to the Carters around the same time. I didn't correct their assumption because it was easier than saying, "Oh, no. It's more a friends-with-bene-fits-with-possibly-a-little-more situation that's com-plicated because I'm also in a similar situationship with an Outer God named Ny, who I'm not introducing you to because it gets even messier."

Ny didn't seem to care he wasn't part of the Carter family festivities. He was cool as always, only say-ing, "Whatever you wish, sweetling," when I hesitantly asked him not to pop in while Mom and Dad were around.

It made me feel like shit though. He was someone I cared about, and I didn't exactly want to hide him away. My parents were accepting and open. Their Mid-western sensibilities would make them not ask too many questions out of fear of being rude. What we had, as two people—well, maybe three people—navigating lust and desire and real feelings I wasn't ready to name yet, would be different for them but also fine.

The magic was the sticking point. They of course knew about me and my early life experiences. We talked about it. It wasn't forbidden conversation or anything. But it was more complicated now, and far more dangerous. I wanted them as far away from the growing magic bits of my life as possible. Harley and Gareth were mages, but they were also human. Merry and Harley were super tight, and the parents had already met Harley via Skype before they even stepped on the plane. They'd also heard of Gareth from Mia's big mouth, which made his appearance a bit of a necessity.

What they didn't know about was Nyarlathotep, Crawling Chaos, the Outer God who shared dream and shadow magic like mine. Ny was sexy as sin, a gracious courtier of sorts who could easily handle parents after navigating the courts of his father for infinity or whatever, but he was a being of magic. Merry and Mia told me they felt it from him. They couldn't sense magic the way I or Harley or Gareth could, but they still felt some otherness crawling across their skin when he popped up. They told me it eased with time and experience, like a mystical form of exposure therapy or something. He tripped my inner magic wire, but he made regular human instincts jump. He was the black lion, a predator of sorts. Mom and Dad would feel his difference, and they weren't stupid. They'd eventually guess what it meant, for me at least, because they knew something about what I could do, and they'd want answers. No way I was getting into what had gone down with Starry Wisdom and the witch house, so I'd asked Ny to step back for a week.

Speaking of Starry Wisdom and the witch house, they had both gone poof. Mia's tabs on the cultist's phone showed radio silence after a time. Harley dug deeper, tried to see if anyone or anything turned up anywhere within her occult circles. Nothing. It seemed, as we'd guessed, Starry Wisdom had disintegrated after the church had popped out of existence, and Macy was gone.

Gone. Dead. Killed, by me. I'd killed Macy. I owned it, but I'd be lying if I said it never bothered me. I was a baker, damnit, not a soldier. Never thought I'd kill someone. I had. Not great, even if necessary. I had John, the familiar, and Macy on my conscience. Gareth, Harley, and Ny had all talked to me about it. They had experience, something I'd guessed at before but got confirmation. We formed a depressing sort of club, I suppose. They all also fully understood why I did what I did. Still, sometimes a flash of red blood on an old wooden floor shot across my vision. Or the crackle of her taunting laugh hit my ears. When those things happened, I had to swallow the bile that rose in my throat at the gnawing memories.

DD helped too. Our bond held, grew even, as I maintained my magic. Ny and Harley wanted me to train more, learn more, but I was tired, hurting. All of it made me hesitant. I didn't give up completely. I also didn't level up in any serious way because I was focused on dealing with all the new, the good and the bad, I'd had thrust into my life in a matter of a few months.

I dealt by baking, like I always had, and running my business. Deb, my business-saving assistant manager, got a promotion and hefty raise after dealing with all my shit when I had too often been out during the whole Starry Wisdom mess. She'd kept everything together, and I loved her for it—and because she was a nice person in general. Always smiling, always patient with colleagues and customers alike. She was a smiling constant in Warm Regards, and I wanted to show how much I appreciated her with the one thing employers should use to show real appreciation: more cash in hand.

My baking assistant, Nate, had also been a lifesaver and somehow baked more quickly and efficiently than I did. I felt and saw his magic daily, but I never pried. I didn't know if he knew, and I wasn't about to enlighten him unless it was absolutely necessary. Harley kept a close eye on him, I think because Merry had a soft spot for him too, so I let it be. We stuck to baking, chatting, and cracking jokes about mundane things while in the kitchen of Warm Regards.

Overall, the summer had been nice. As we steered firmly into the heat of August, I was content. Mostly. The major sticking point beyond my guilt was Mia.

She'd got back to quasi-normal after the Necronom-icon thing, but something was off with her and she refused to talk about it. Her sassy shine had dulled. Oh, she went through the motions, trying to convince me and everyone else she was all good. Her eyes told a different story. Sometimes they stared off as if focused on something not visible to anyone else. I swear, a few times their dark-brown shade darkened—like literally bled from brown to an almost-black color, before she'd close them, shake her head, and be good. Freaked me out when I saw it, but she insisted it was nothing, not to worry, and all that jazz. DD rattled in an odd way when she did it, so I knew bone deep she was in some serious shit. Shit she probably couldn't fully deal with on her own.

Merry and I had given her space at first because we felt she'd needed it. They were kind enough to give it to me when my mind wandered to Macy, so I was determined to return the favor to Mia. To be brutally honest, it was also what I needed. A break. As summer heated up and edged toward fall, it was getting harder and harder to ignore she wasn't dealing. Space was all well and good, but sometimes crowding was necessary, and I could tell it was about time for my youngest sister. We had given her nearly two months, an eternity in nosy-Carter-sister time. A come-to-Jesus talk was in order, and Merry and I would give it to her soon.

Before I could do that, however, Ny decided I needed my own talking-to. Too bad for him he'd chosen a bad time to do it.

I'd spent a long day in my kitchen. A long day baking in the humid heat of an Ohio August, to be precise. Definitely not fun times, regardless of my enjoyment of baking. It was still work and still ungodly hot to do in late summer. I'd baked all day, prepping a massive birthday cupcake tower order for delivery the next day. Dozens and dozens of pineapple, strawberry, and lemon cupcakes had been topped with fluffy mountains of vanilla buttercream and sprinkled with edible glitter. There would be a happy little girl excited about her huge party and pretty cupcakes the next day, but it wasn't the easiest work to do with temps in the 90s and humidity stretched higher.

All this to say I was tired, slightly annoyed, and ready for a cool shower and some dinner when I found Ny leaning against my apartment door.

I gave a weak smile and said, "I hope this isn't business, because I'm too tired for any magic nonsense."

Ny straightened as I moved forward, and he took me in his arms as soon as I was close enough. "I'd say it was always all pleasure with you, sweetling, but we both know that's a lie," he said before giving me a quick but heated kiss.

I wanted the kiss to linger, to lead to more. My magic even rose to meet it, but I pulled back with a sigh. His words weren't an assurance he was here for sexy good times, and Ny always made his intentions clear from the beginning. Something else was obviously up. "Come in," I groused, pushing him aside slightly to enter my apartment and the AC haven it provided.

I slouched toward my kitchen bar, hopped on a stool, and rolled my neck and shoulders. They were tight as hell from baking all day. "Out with it, Ny."

He pulled up behind me and rubbed my shoulders, digging in just enough to give a small slice of pain, the only real way to get the knots out during a massage. I couldn't help it. I gave a deep moan at his touch, both from the way it felt and the memories it provided.

"I do wish to take you up on the offer, sweet Randy," Ny whispered in my ear before he straightened and came back to his full voice. "However, there are issues we must address."

"Of course there are," I grumbled, twisting myself so his hands dropped from my shoulders and I could face him. "Again, out with it."

"Our training should resume."

"I know," I said, maybe a little whiny. "I'm just tired."

Ny stepped up and cupped my cheek. "Of course you are. And all is still new to you. Plus, we have had a number of weeks without incident, which makes training seem unnecessary."

"But preparation is half the job," I said, repurposing an old pastry school motto for magic.

"Exactly. Starry Wisdom is gone, yet Wilbur remains. As does the entity backing him."

"The one who still holds your power," I replied, stepping off the stool to give him a tight squeeze. "I'm sorry, Ny. You've been so gracious and helpful, and I haven't really done anything to help you out, which is pretty shitty of me."

"No, sweetling. Time is relative to me. I do not think it wasted when it is spent with you. However, being in my full power would give me, and you, certain advantages. It would also make any threats moot."

"That much power, huh?"

A sly, cocky smile spread on his lips, but he said nothing in reply.

"Okay. What's your suggestion? I'm sure you came with one."

"Indeed, I did. I think it best we return to dream-walking training, and we bring Gareth into the fold."

It was something Ny had brought up before. Something Gareth had also discussed. All of it also centered around more than magic, or actually, a very different type of magic I'd never really used for any effect before. "By bringing Gareth into the fold, you mean..."

"In training only. We are all adults. We all know the sex magic the three of us could produce would be beneficial for any end. Something we definitely should explore. But I would never push you into such a thing if you were not interested."

Damnit, I was interested. Who wouldn't be? Gareth, big-guy calm, against the crackle of Ny's dark energy and lean-muscled body. I knew it'd be explosive. The issue was whether it would make us explode in a good or bad way. To be honest, losing either or changing our relationship in a fundamental way scared me.

"I know, I know." I shook my head, took a deep breath, and jumped. "We do need to start training again. We also need Gareth involved. In training, I mean. For now."

"Very well. Do you wish to contact Gareth and make arrangements?"

"Yes. After I take a shower and relax for a bit."

"Whatever you need." His nod was so deep, it could've been a bow. Sensing the unspoken part of my request for alone time, he said, "Text me the plan," before he stepped closer again and gave a soft, sweet kiss to my forehead. With a wink and a grin, he walked to the nearest shadow and faded from sight, going wherever it was he went when he wasn't hanging around me.

I slumped and shuffled toward my bathroom, feeling guilty. I hadn't told Ny about what I'd been dreaming. Hadn't told anyone, in fact. And I probably should've.

Two

ABOUT THOSE NEWER DREAMS. To give myself some credit, they definitely weren't dream walking, not in the strictest sense of the term. Who was I kidding? I didn't really know enough about dream walking to be an expert on it, which was why I should've talked to Ny and Gareth about it sooner.

First odd thing was it was a recurring dream, one that played out exactly the same way every night I had it, and I'd had it most nights by the end of summer. It had started slow, only once a week or so, but had ramped up quickly. The fact it had the same events, in the same order, with no changes, made me think it was a regular old dream. My dream walks to the black church and the witch house had been similar, sure, but never exactly the same. Events shifted and changed because I reacted to what was occurring in the dream walk. That was not the same with this dream.

This new dream started with me coming into consciousness in a dark cave. Maybe the cave was carved from black stone, or maybe it was so dark, I only saw black stone. Either way, all I could see was blackness with the occasional glints of odd silver flashing across the stone, as if there was some tiny light source I couldn't pinpoint sliding over the surfaces. The walls, the ceiling, the floor. It was all made from this same stuff.

I could feel it too. Another shift from my dream walks. I would walk over and touch the wall, feeling its intentionally smoothed surface and its hardness on my hands without passing through. Same with my feet as I walked. Barefoot, they'd thud across the floor making solid contact.

Like the black church dreams, I would be dressed in an ancient-looking black robe. The fabric would drift over me in waves, seeming to move in a non-existent wind. It snagged on my curves—my breasts, my rounded belly, my full ass and thighs—creating fabric shadows over my body, as if it were a part of my body rather than the shadows usually attracted to my body. It was an odd distinction I felt but couldn't explain.

Speaking of my shadows, they never showed there. DD was nowhere in sight in these dreams. No hovering ball bouncing at my peripheral vision. The only shadows I could make out were the inky, tentacle-like blackness clinging to the sharp angle where the ceiling met the wall, the same shadows I felt and used in the witch house. They had slithered out of the crack in space and time Macy and Wilbur had created. In my dream, it gyrated and pulsed, occasionally reaching shadow tentacles down toward me but never far enough to touch me.

Dream-me never panicked, at least not outwardly. I noticed in my head and skittered away mentally, but dream-me moved forward to where the cave began to slope downward. Down into a deeper darkness I somehow navigated without falling all over myself, like a dark room I knew so well I didn't need to turn on the light to get through it.

When the slope ended, I'd find myself in front of a swirling well made from the same dark stone as the rest of the cave-like structure. It rose from the floor like a natural feature. There weren't any bricks or seams I could see. It was as smooth and honed as the rest of the place, almost like the entire thing had been dug out, carved, and smoothed to create a massive space to house this small well about four feet high and three feet wide.

I'd stop, look in the well, and see swirling shadows like the tentacles still clinging above. They were a mass of undulating things, lapping and turning in a big, endless ball of darkness. I couldn't see a beginning or end, only the constant turning and moving of the things. Then, a single tentacle would reach out of the mass up toward me, a piece of metal glinting in the low light wrapped up in its suckered fist. I'd stand frozen, my body calmly watching and waiting while my working mind screamed for me to get away, run, do whatever it took to not let this thing touch me. Dream-me never listened. I'd reach out a finger, pointing toward the shadow as it stretched out the shiny metal thing around the slick darkness of the shadow itself. It would get about an inch from my hand, ready to give me whatever it held and dream-me ready to take it, when I'd wake up—usually in a sweat, breathing hard and heavy and blinking wildly for long minutes.

Maybe it was a regular person's nightmare or something dredged up by my anxiety over coming to terms with my magic and power. Maybe it was some Freudian thing I should've looked up in a dream book. I had a suspicion it was something else entirely, something new and likely important, but like so much with me and my magic, I shoved it away out of fear of change. I was hoping one day the toxic trait would be conquered, but I wouldn't hold my breath until then.

Whatever the case, it all ended up the same: I buried my head in the sand and didn't tell anyone about these dreams, doing my best oblivious-ostrich impression.

AFTER NY'S LITTLE AMBUSH, some much-needed rest, and a smooth delivery of birthday cupcakes—without a kidnapping attempt—I prepped for a different kind of party. It was family meal at Warm Regards.

Family meal was something I'd loved when I worked in the larger food industry. There, it had happened far more often. Sometimes it was about using up leftovers from a particular menu, sometimes it was a bonding event. Whatever the case, family meal was a time outside of peak business for all the people in a restaurant or catering place to come together and eat food they prepared, not for customers but for each other. It was a time to commune and show off in equal measure.

Warm Regards had its own family meal sporadically, and it'd been well over six months since the last family meal. Not that I didn't want to do it more, but a bakery didn't produce a lot of meal-like leftovers, and things had been hectic, what with my time being split between baking and doing magical things. With things on the magic front being calmer, I decided family meal was a priority.

Employees generally ate whatever they wanted from the bakery. I knew the few people working every day wouldn't eat me out of business, and it seemed better to let them have their sugar fix whenever they wanted to have it. Plus, they and my sisters were the usual taste-testers for my new flavors and ideas, so I liked giving them my normal bakes or baking experiments on a semi-regular basis. All this meant my normal bakery-café fare was standard for everyone who'd be at family meal. Because of this, I always did something different and special.

It was hot, it was summer, and I wanted to go all out, so I did homemade pasta— fettuccine to be precise—with an easy butter and parmesan cheese sauce dotted with bright English peas and mushrooms. It was light, fit everyone's needs, and showed off another flour-based thing I could do besides tasty sweet treats.

My employee roster had grown to eight people, not including me—six café workers, Deb the manager, and my baking assistant, Nate. Not a lot compared to other businesses, but growth all the same. I included Merry and Mia in family meal because I loved them, but they also did a lot of free work for me. Merry with her financial things and Mia as my social media guru. Eleven people total for family meal—not huge but a solid number.

I planned it for after hours, then told everyone they were invited and I'd provide the bulk of the food, so they didn't feel pressure to cook or to come at all. All eleven decided to come, though most did opt out of cooking. Deb said she'd bring a big salad—a good call given the pasta and the weather. Nate wanted to stretch his baking more and show how he did things, so he claimed dessert. Merry and Mia came with a tricked-out charcuterie board. Yasmiin brought Somali sambusa, a deliciously fried, flaky triangle filled with fragrant, spiced ground beef. It was a good time with good people, and we enjoyed everything presented.

Merry sat next to Nate, her beautiful oval face full of laughter as Nate told some story he punctuated with wild gesticulations of his hands, his lush and shining brown hair and eyes glinting in the soft café lighting. Merry whipped her head quickly to the side, her dark-brown hair streaming, to include Mia in the conversation. My littlest sister smiled, even chuckled, but it didn't reach her dark-brown eyes. She was colder, more distant. Her short hair was styled, her easy nerd-girl look the same, but the bags were still there under her eyes. She'd just gotten really good with concealer. I could see them, faint purplish bruises telling me of sleepless nights. Merry turned back toward Nate, but the tension of her shoulders caught my attention. We needed to have a chat with Mia, and soon.

Deb brought me out of my deeper thoughts. "You seem less distracted lately. If I had two hot dudes showing up to spend time with me, I'd be a little more distracted."

I turned my head to my assistant manager, a lifeline in a very different, but no less real and important area of my life—my business—and slung my arm over her seat back. "Your organizational skills would have Gareth and Ny in quick order, on a regular rotation, if they were in your life."

Deb laughed. "True. I like my schedules."

"I love you for it because I have no head for them."

"Nope," she said.

I looked at her with an exaggerated squint. "You're lucky your boss is so easy-going. Not many would tolerate this sort of backtalk."

She huffed. "I know you and the rest of the Carter family. You respect a little backtalk and sass."

"Too true again," I said, "but how am I going to make you fear me and therefore do better work?"

She flung her head toward the bakery case behind us. "You use sugar. Much more effective."

In the din of chatter, the laughter, in the midst of teasing, I felt a moment of happiness and gratitude well up in me, particularly for this woman. "You're the best, Deb. You know that?"

She shrugged but I pushed. "No. Really. Things got a little weird this spring and summer. You held down the fort, so to speak. Took care of all the day-to-day so I could focus on baking when I could. Without you..." I trailed off, not knowing what to say. Without her, I'd have probably lost the bakery because I'd have been unable to pay my bills. My magical abilities were important, sure, but so were the practical things. I couldn't fully commit to saving people from evil cults or half gods if I was worried about a place to live or where I'd get my next meal. Even beyond the practical, baking was a part of me, just like my magic. I loved it, deep down to my core, and Deb's work helped me keep doing what I loved.

I shook off the morose thoughts and smiled widely at her. "You saved me."

"Not all heroes wear capes," she quipped, deflecting the praise in the offhand way she normally did while serving a beaming smile. "Now that I've reached hero status, I'll need to find me a couple of hot hero-wor-shipping groupies. Gareth and Ny have any brothers?"

I snorted. Gareth was an only child. Ny, not quite, but I doubted Deb wanted to start seeing any of the other Outer Gods. "You're better off with Tinder."

"Ugh," she said. "No thanks. I'll hold out hope some charmer will come in here and sweep me off my feet."

I raised my beer to tap the neck of hers. "Here's to hope." In more ways than one.

Three

AFTER THE THIRD NIGHT in a row with my weird cave dream, which just happened to coincide with my convo with Ny about more dream-walker training à la *Dream Warriors* or whatever he had in mind, I called Harley. Not like I didn't talk to Harley on the regular or anything. She was dating my sister. We had family things together. We also talked about magic and occultish stuff. She gave me pointers and told me about helpful research or source materials, even if she wasn't strictly showing me the ropes anymore. We were magic colleagues of a sort, and friends. And, really, family. In more ways than one. Going through serious shit with a person creates a connection that was a bit outside a lot of other names a relationship can have.

Anyway, I called her specifically to discuss the dreams, because I knew she was a good sounding board. Of course, after telling her about the cave and the shadow tentacles and the odd solidness-but-uncontrollable aspect of it all, she started with, "You need to discuss your dreams with the Prince."

I decided to deflect. "Why did you call him the Prince?"

"He is, right? It's his official title."

"Yes, but it's so..."

"Real," Harley said with a firm tone. "It's real, Randy. Nyarlathotep is the Prince of the Dreamlands, a creature at the center of creation. He's into you, for sure. He appears to be genuine and helpful, and maybe he truly is, but only because of you and what he sees in you or knows he can have from you. He's still an Outer God. It'd be best we *all* remember that, at least from time to time."

"Doesn't sound like the type of person I should chat with about my dreams," I grumbled.

"The opposite, actually. He's exactly who you should talk to about these dreams. First, because he's old as dirt, older even, and knows far more than any of us ever could about the magic you have. Second, I suspect he'd rip the universe apart to keep you safe, and anything hinting at impending danger for you should be discussed with him."

I blew out a harsh breath. Maybe all Harley said was true, but it was a hard truth. I still squirmed a bit under the pressure of my magic and the unanswered questions about who or what I was in the grand scheme of things. "Okay. I hear you. I do. I'm still asking for your opinion. You know an awful lot about magic too, you know."

"I know," she said with her firm confidence. "I'm the shit, but even someone as good as me has their limits. I'm only human."

"A human who's halted their aging and harnessed the most powerful of spells in my presence."

"All right. All right. Enough flattery." She paused, and I could almost picture her on her phone, leaning against something, her free hand buried deep in a trouser pocket and her face, dark, stark cheekbones and piercing brown eyes, pinched in serious thought.

Finally, she spoke. "You're right to assume they aren't dream walks. Doesn't sound like any dream walk description I've ever heard. Add in the fact you feel conscious but out of control and I'd say they were standard recurring nightmares. You've had a load of traumatic events go down in pretty quick succession. But..."

"But what?" I pressed, needed her ideas. Maybe just to reassure myself.

"But the solid feeling, the sensations you describe? Not typical dream behavior. It gives me pause."

"Me too," I whispered so lightly into the phone I didn't know if she even heard it.

"Talk to Ny and Gareth. Trust their expertise."

"Will do," I said with more confidence. I didn't necessarily like it, but I was done with avoidance. Too much shit had gone down in the past six-ish months to think avoidance was the best course of action in any situation. My ostrich tendencies were disengaged, for the moment.

"Randy," Harley said with a warmer tone. "I do like you to come to me with these issues."

"I'll continue to do it too. No getting rid of me."

"Good. I have to go."

I chuckled at her abrupt turn, but it was so her. No-nonsense and to the point.

"Hot date?"

"Don't think you want to hear about my hot dates with Merry."

"Too true. I'll let you go."

"Bye." Then the phone clicked and those universal beeps signaled the call ended.

Okay then. I'd gotten some info from Harley, but most of it along the same train of thought I'd had. I needed to talk to Ny and Gareth. Good thing I'd already set all that up for the next afternoon.

THE GUYS SHOWED UP at my place to work in my storage-turned-training room the next night. Both looked the usual. Gareth in loose jeans, a tee tight across his bulging muscles, his sigil tats on full display, and his beard trimmed for summer and his blond hair tied back securely in a low man-bun. Ny in a black leather jacket, a white shirt clinging to his lean muscle underneath, and tight dark jeans slung low enough bits of his light-brown skin played peekaboo with his hem when he moved. His hair, black and floppy and slightly spiky around the crown, was artfully pushed back from his face without help from any product I could detect, which seemed like its own bit of magic. They were gorgeous, yummy even, in their own unique ways. Enough to make a girl's choice hard. If she had to choose.

Talk and action on all sides, as of now, pointed to the fact I didn't have to choose. So why was I still hesitant, not reveling in having my cake and eating it too? A bit of fear of what would happen with our dynamic and a dash of stubbornness mainly. Plus, as worldly and open as I was, as sexually open as I was, I hadn't ever actually had more than one partner at a time. Much less more than one partner at a time at the same time, which seemed to be the direction we were all taking. Tantalizing? Yes. A bit scary given all the moving parts—physically, emotionally, and magically? Most definitely.

Ny'd told me more about sex magic over the course of our summer in and out of bed. We created it every time we were together, the black floating star-dotted mini piece of outer space. I'd also paid more attention to the same with Gareth, noticing the light and flair of his sigils glow stronger with each encounter, sensing the shadows in my churn to the beat of his sexy calm more readily. I was compatible with each in their own way, our bodies and magics weaving together to prove it time and time again. I knew if we harnessed the power, it may be useful in the future. Besides, how we got to the harnessing bit would likely be lots of sexy good times. Still, I held back, afraid the delicate bubble of care and connection we'd created over the past few months would burst if we took the leap.

Don't get it twisted. Just because I was hesitant to make sex a group activity, didn't mean I wasn't putting on a show for either man when I knew they'd be around. I was still having sex with each, smile maybe not as often as anyone liked. To that end, I was dressed for a workout with a small dash of seduction thrown in for good measure. My low-cut tank highlighted my cleavage and hugged the curves of my breasts snuggly so they had good heft while still giving a soft bounce when I walked. My tummy, definitely not flat, was smoothed a touch but not hidden. These men knew every part of me, enjoyed my body as much as I did, so I didn't want to hide or minimize. My cropped leggings showed all the dips and curves and valleys of my ass and hips. With my midnight-black hair pulled up and my pale face and navy eyes makeup free, I was a midsize queen in training mode—looking and feeling sexy, while also ready to rumble. A good combo in my book. Seemed a good combo for Gareth and Ny as well, as heat hit their eyes when I opened the door to my apartment stairs.

"Hey there," I said with a happy lilt to my voice. I was genuinely happy to see them. Each made me feel in different ways—Gareth with his calm aura and Ny with his sizzling flashes of power—and I enjoyed all those sensations.

Gareth gave a quick head-to-toe and a slow, seductive smile peeked out from his beard. "Hello, Randy." He moved in for a quick hug, squeezing my body to his hard form before stepping back far enough to let Ny pop his head in the door frame.

"No hug for me? I'm hurt, sweetling," Ny said as he pulled his face into an exaggerated pout.

Damn if that wasn't also sexy, with his regal face turned down, his full lips pursed. I wanted to kiss the sadness away. "Oh, stop," I huffed, smacking him playfully in the chest before pulling him into a quick but hard embrace. "No time for pouting. You're the one who pressed about starting this thing up."

"Yes, I did," he said, bringing a long-fingered hand up to grab a piece of hair from my ponytail and play with it gently in a distracted manner. He cut eyes back to Gareth, who stood a step behind. "In regard to a number of things."

Heat hit my cheeks at his allusion to the exact thing I'd been thinking of before their arrival.

Speaking of their arrival. "Wait. Did you guys come here together?"

"No," Gareth answered, narrowing the gap between him and Ny half a step so they crowded me farther into the stairway. "Ny was leaning against the building in his usual cool manner when I pulled up."

"I've come to anticipate Gareth's arrivals. He's normally early to all meetings, yet only by a few minutes so as to not be a burden," Ny said with an aloof shrug.

I was curious how he was learning so much about Gareth. But all these innuendos and questions could wait for later. I acknowledged Ny's admission with a nod and turned, saying over my shoulder, "Come on, then. If we're doing this thing, let's get to it." I bounced up the stairs, feeling both men's eyes on my ass as I climbed, letting their gazes send a thrill of lust down my spine before I squirreled it away and attempted to follow my own directions to do the damn thing.

This thing was the business of dream-walker training. After letting the guys into my training space and waving to each to sit on the soft rug Ny had left there on our first session, I joined them on the floor. DD bounced around, excited to return to the shadow plane. I gave it a thumbs-up and a grin before I turned my attention to Ny. "How's this supposed to work?"

His look was serious, no longer leaking sexy and smug energy. He could turn all business in a split second, something I appreciated about the Outer God. These types of actions said he liked good times, but business was business and was to be taken seriously.

"The theory is the same. We meditate together, connect, and assume our joined power will guide us to a dream-like state together as it did when there were only two of us."

"Will my lack of internal magic be a roadblock?" Gareth asked, his eyes on Ny and his brows creased in thought. As business-like as Ny was, Gareth was too, but in a slightly different vein. His came from curiosity, questions, a need to understand. All very librarian-mage of him and an attitude I admired.

"Do you currently have reserves?" Ny asked in return.

Gareth didn't answer with words. He blinked rapidly, which did something to make a series of sigils on his forearms glow slightly.

"Good. Yet..." Ny bent slightly forward, as we were in a crude three-person circle of sorts on the floor, and tapped one of the sigils glowing on Gareth's arm. It flared brighter and darker all at once, a visual contradiction only believable because Ny's magic, maybe even my magic, was present.

Gareth's forearms flexed at the charge in power. "I will never get used to that feeling," he muttered, reminding me of how he'd taken Ny's power back at the witch house earlier in the summer. He'd taken so much then, he'd been able to use Ny's darkness when he'd fought Wilbur.

"Merely a touch, friend. To help us connect in case a similar flavor of magic is required for us to unite."

We zipped it after Ny's zap, focusing inward to get to the meditation plane. I popped into my kitchen happy space pretty damn quickly after all my practice. Ny still beat me there, lounging against a worktable with all his regal feline grace.

"So…"

"We wait," Ny said. "For a time. Gareth's never inhabited your space. It may take some effort on his part."

Luckily for us, not much effort. Though his appearance was odd. "Why's he all hollow looking?" I asked Ny as I peeked through Gareth's barely-there body a few minutes later. He looked a little like the shades Ny had shown me in the cemetery when we'd first started training.

"Why are you solid?" Gareth asked.

Ny flicked his hand as if it was all no big deal. "We are shadow magic and therefore can flit wholly in and out of realms. Gareth, however, cannot. Only part of him can enter this space."

"Because we have shadow magic we can go anywhere?"

"I did not say 'have.' I said 'are.' It is an important distinction. You are like me in the fact your being is made of shadow magic. We do not simply wield it."

"Which makes you more adept at adaptation, transfiguration, and interdimensional movement," Gareth said, his own knowledge and experience filling in the blanks. Good for him, but it left me a little out of the loop.

"Does this mean I can travel wherever, whenever? Like 'poof' I'm in Paris. Or even a multiverse version of Paris?"

"Not exactly, sweetling. You need knowledge, access, and practice. In theory, you would be able to more readily travel in various forms and planes, like with shadow walking and dream walking."

That was a nice tidbit of knowledge to tuck away for later, but it didn't exactly help with the issue of training, which was why the three of us were there. Gesturing toward Gareth's filmy form, I said, "Will this be an issue for whatever it is you think we should be doing together?'

"No, lovely. Mainly because we are already doing it. For now."

I cocked my head, and once again, Gareth filled in the blanks. "The first training test had to be whether we could all inhabit the same space outside the human realm at will. No sense training with all three of us if I couldn't get to the same places as everyone else."

"Randy also needed practice pulling someone else other than me into a meditative or dream space, so there was that, but yes. Before all else, we needed to know it was possible."

More than a little defensive, I said, "A heads-up might be nice next time."

"Oh, sweetling. Don't be cross," Ny said, coming to stand close and hug my body to his. He kissed the hollow of my neck, a whisper-soft feeling of lips across my skin. I shivered from the touch but looked over toward Gareth to gauge his reaction. He stood tall and still, his usual small smile in place.

I shook out of the moment and said, "I won't be cross when you let me in on the details beforehand."

Ny squeezed my waist and pulled back to give me a serious expression. "Consider it done." And it would be, because Ny didn't play games with me. When he said it would happen, I could trust it would happen.

"Good," I said, jutting my chin out before turning fully toward Gareth. "How do you feel here? Is it different than when you dream walk?"

"I'm solid in my own dream walks, but not here. I suppose because you pulled me in. We may need to try again. As I've now been to this space, I need to see if I can will myself here."

The next hour was spent meditating, talking, and practicing. It took Gareth several attempts, but he finally arrived in my meditative space in all his calming solidness and could even use magic there. I called it a win and a day. Ny agreed but said we needed more practice. Gareth shrugged and went with the flow, as per usual. I came back to my training room a final time, and was alone for a few beats before Gareth and Ny appeared between blinks, their spaces empty one millisecond and filled the next as if they'd always been there.

I rolled my shoulders and twisted my neck to stretch before asking, "When should we meet up again?"

"I say soon, but not to practice," Gareth answered.

I looked at him with my head cocked in question and Ny said, "We chatted for a moment before we returned, sweetling. Gareth and I would very much like it if you'd agree to go on a date. With both of us."

"For real?" I got serious nods all around. We'd hedged this issue for a while. Looked like the dudes were no longer waiting for me to make the move.

"Just a date?"

"Oh, I'm sure we both hope for more than dinner," Ny said with a sly grin, "but yes. A dinner date with all three of us in attendance."

I tingled at the thought of more, desire and trepidation both present in my mind and body. Looking at each man, I tried to gauge how they might actually feel about all this, but mind reading was sadly not a power I had. I needed to trust this was what they wanted, and I needed a no-pressure test to see if it was what I wanted too.

"Okay. Dinner for three. I can't do tomorrow night because I'm hanging with Merry and Mia. Sister time is sacred. The night after works, and I'm not picking the place. You two can handle the details."

Gareth's smirk was different than Ny's, less feline and more in line with the human masculine variety, but it was no less potent. "I'll handle it, Randy. Don't you worry."

Four

THE HANG WITH MERRY and Mia was less a chill sister hangout and more an intervention. We'd all given Mia room to deal with her issues and come to us for help. Hell, Merry and I had been covering for her with Mom and Dad since they'd hit town this summer, making excuses about her off behavior.

On one level, I got it. More than Merry did. Magic shit was messed up, especially once I learned a lot about it. Merry was my anchor, true. She dealt with experiencing my dreams vicariously, and for a while those dreams were not fun to even vicariously experience. She also dated Harley and spent a lot of time at her place, which can only be described as Batman's condo but make it magic instead of gadgets. It would be unfair to say Merry didn't know anything about magic.

But she didn't feel it, experience it, have it rooted inside her. I had a sneaking suspicion Mia's problem wasn't that the book she'd hunted down in the bowels of the internet had shown her some messed-up stuff, but it had actually done some messed-up stuff. To her.

Changed her in some way. Wilbur's ominous threats and a few chats with Harley earlier in the summer had confirmed my fears.

It'd been two-ish months. Summer was barreling toward fall. We'd given her space. Now, she needed us to get into her face. If I was right, and the book had changed her, we had to deal with whatever the change was before it burst out and got real messy. Hence, the movie night at my place, which was actually an intervention.

Merry and I were waiting on the couch, trying not to look like angry parents up to catch a kid missing curfew, when Mia rolled into my place. She didn't burst through the door, a little tornado of nerdy energy and sass, like she would've a few months before. She carried her laptop in with her, the bag nearly sliding off her slightly hunched shoulder. The dark circles under her eyes were more prominent than they had been at family meal, and her short dark hair was slightly greased and tight to her skull. She looked worse than she had in a while, which made my heart lurch. The intervention was definitely the best call.

After thumping the laptop bag on the dining room table like it were a sack of flour, Mia finally eyed our positions with a hint of weariness. "What's up?" she asked, leaning against the edge of the table and facing us with arms crossed over her chest rather than coming to sit in the living room. Defensive posture from the jump, it seemed.

"How are you doing, Mia?" Merry asked instead of outright answering, using her soothing voice to try to smooth out Mia's ruffles.

"Had a long day. Just finished work and raced over here to relax with my sisters, but," she said as her eyes bounced between us, "looks like something else might be going on."

"Oh?" I asked, my one attempt at easing into the conversation.

"'Oh' yes," she said with a snap, a trace of Mia's familiar and sometimes loveable snark coloring her voice. "No snacks, no movie cued up, no comfy clothes and laughs. Just…" She gestured up and down at us. I couldn't blame her. The apartment wasn't screaming relaxing night with sisters. Two of the three sisters in question sat plank straight, plastered to each other's sides. I was even wearing my training gear for some god-awful reason I didn't want to think too much about at the moment. Granted, my training gear was basically athleisurewear because no one sold shadow and dream magic practice clothes, but still. Beside me, Merry was wearing her summer standard: a knee-length flowy dress highlighting her ethereal, nymph-like beauty. The beauty was marred a bit by the way she clenched her hands in her lap, her grip on the light fabric so tight her knuckles clearly strained against her taut skin.

"Okay, look. Let's not dance around this. We need to talk. More specifically, *you* need to talk."

Merry jumped in with a little more finesse and sweetness. "Mia, honey. What's going on? You're not yourself. Haven't been for a while."

"It's the book." I leaned toward her, putting my elbows to my knees. "We all know it's the book. You know we know it's the book, and every single one of us needs to stop playing this game of pretend where we don't talk about the massive elephant-sized book in the room."

Mia sucked in a breath and closed her eyes. "I can't. Not yet."

"Obviously!" I yelled, jumping up to pace.

"Randy," Merry said with warning, trying to calm me down. And she was right to calm me. I wasn't mad at Mia. Not exactly. I was worried. Beyond worried—terrified about whatever had happened to my baby sister. As I tried to shake off the pent-up frustration oozing out as anger, Merry continued. "Mia, you don't have to tell us everything. We're not demanding you bare your soul to us, sis, but it's been months. You've struggled on your own with this. It's time to let some of the burden go. Time for us to carry the weight."

Mia chose to dig in. "I'm fine."

"You can lie to others, maybe even lie to yourself, but you can't lie about it to us. Not us." I shifted my pace to walk toward her. "It was less than six months ago my worldview was spectacularly blown up. You two nosed your way in and made me deal with it—the magic and you helping me. What makes you think we're not going to do the same for you?"

Mia swallowed hard and said, "You can't help."

I snorted in disagreement but Merry gently replied, "You don't know that for sure until you let us try."

There was a slight tremor to Mia's whisper when she said, "I do know, because the book told me."

"The book told you? Like literally talked to you?"

She looked up, stark pain and fear screaming at me from her once-lovely round face, and said, "Talks. Still talks to me."

I stopped in front of my sister, my heart beating a mile a minute, though I took the time to calm my face. "Talk to *US*, Mia. Please." She hugged herself, her petite frame not looking like the confident midtwenties badass I knew her to be but like a frightened animal, shying away from something I didn't fully understand.

I pulled out two chairs and sat Mia down. She avoided my eyes but allowed me to guide her. "Sis. It's time you told us what's going on. At least part of it."

Merry came to take a seat at the table as Mia, slumping farther down into her chair, began to speak.

"You know about the Necronomicon, what it is. Why and how I looked for it." We did. Mia had discovered the existence of the book—a book of spells so powerful it was rarely seen or read and there hadn't been a complete copy of it around in over a century. However, through her exploration of dark web occultist chatter, Mia had discovered that the book, once completed, would hold the key to understanding shadow magic specifically, something I could definitely use. My little sister had done it for me, compiled digital bits and pieces of this super powerful spell book to potentially help with the magic mess I'd been mired in at the time. We'd seen it affect her and told her to stop, but something had happened. Something about the book had changed Mia, and we weren't entirely sure what the change was or how it'd happened. To be sure, Mia needed to talk to us, so I was happy to let her continue.

"Well, you told me to stop, for totally valid reasons. And I did. For a day. Something made me keep searching and compiling even though I promised I wouldn't. It was like a compulsion. I couldn't get the book out of my head, what we could do with it, how helpful it could be."

"We know, Mia, and it's okay," I interjected to offer at least a small comfort as she told us more.

"I got it. As in, I have a completed electronic version of the Necronomicon. More than likely the first full electronic version in history. Maybe even the only full version in existence as of right now."

"Okay, honey. You completed the book. What exactly did it do?" Merry asked.

"That's the thing. I completed the book. It took a part of me to get the last pieces in place, kind of like I molded myself to fit in the wholes where missing jigsaw pieces were supposed to go. And I gave up the small bits of me willingly, cramming it where it was needed and letting the whole picture form. In exchange, the text lodged itself in my head once it was finished, fusing with my mind somehow."

"Shit," I said, plopping back into my chair. Wilbur had said she'd completed it, and I'd worried about what he'd hinted at for months. "Okay, so you completed the book. Walk us through what it means."

"Okay. You know I had to piecemeal the thing, dig into really dark and scary parts of the internet to get it." When we nodded, she continued. "Some of the pieces were locked behind electronic wards and spells, but those weren't too hard for me to get around with my regular skills. Seems mages aren't too knowledgeable when it comes to electronic security, even if they have magic to help. It was work, don't get me wrong, but nothing I couldn't handle. The text itself, well, the little I read haunted me, tugged at my brain in the weirdest way. It was scary but also called to me? I can't fully explain it. It was like I was repelled and pulled in at the same time.

"The last bit, the final scanned pages to the book, were different from all the rest. They were just there, hidden in some odd folder in the dark recesses of someone's database. I was obsessed, in a frenzy to get the book together. It wasn't even fully about Randy anymore, about helping her. Part of it still was, sure, but most of it was for myself by then, my own weird need to have all of this book in front of me, to learn its secrets."

She stopped, shame filling the lines of her face. I couldn't help it, I had to touch her, comfort her, so I pulled her to me, in a tight, quick embrace, telling her, "It's okay. Go on, sis. Give us the rest."

She shook, her body and her voice, but she gave it all to us. "It's hard to even explain what happened. It's magic, you know? All wonky and otherworldly and working against all the standard practices of the universe. Anyway, I found the last of the pages the night before y'all took out the witch. They... whispered to me. Told me what to do from the screen, how to free them. I did it. I said words, spilled a little of my own blood, and felt a piece of myself, something deep in my mind, tear free. The hole wasn't there for long. A shard of something else, something unknowable and inhuman, embedding itself there like code I can't erase. It's been stuck there ever since, a dark voice in my head saying horrible, horrible things."

She shuddered, tears rolling down her face, and I didn't ask for specifics, although I knew those would come. With the others—Harley and Ny and Gareth—specifics would be important. It'd be how they'd know exactly what happened and what we could do to fix it. Now wasn't about fixing it. Merry I and knew this going into tonight. The intervention was about talking it out, and Mia had clearly talked enough. However, there were a few practical concerns we had to go over.

"Have you read more of the book? Where is it now?" Surely getting her away from it would help alleviate some of this until we had a more solid plan.

"Can't help but read. Every night. I pour over the pages. Have to or I can't get the little bit of sleep I do manage."

"So, we take it, right?" Merry asked. "Harley probably knows where we could hide it."

Mia shook her head. "You don't understand. It's electronic, not physical. It exists only in digital form, and the digital form is connected to me and me alone. You can't hide it away because it's everywhere. On my laptop, my phone, my television. It creeps in through the radio of my car. It's everywhere for me and nowhere for anyone else."

She was crying then, big body-shaking sobs of pain and exhaustion. Merry and I huddled around her, letting her cry between us. There was little we could do otherwise. I barely had a grasp on my own magic, let alone digital-magic hybrids I'd never even heard about. It hurt more than I could say, more than being ripped apart the first time I shadow walked, to see my little sister like that. I'd held her as a bawling baby, taken care of her scraped knees and broken hearts, helped her learn to ride a bike and drive a car. To know I couldn't immediately help with this much-more-severe problem was a slice to the gut, an undoing in its own way. I kept those feelings locked down tight though. This wasn't about my emotions. Today's focus was on Mia.

I pulled back when her crying began to taper some. "Look at me, Mia."

When her pain-filled brown eyes met my navy ones, I put my own magic forward to let her see I'd put all the power I had behind her. I knew my eyes held stars, not as vast as Ny's but somewhat similar. They shared a piece of dark shadow with the Outer God and conveyed a whole lot of fuck-around-and-find-out vibes. Mia needed to see it in me, know I spoke as her sister and as something a little bit more. "We will figure this out. We'll get Harley and Gareth and Ny on this, and they'll know what to do. How to help. We'll all do whatever it takes to help. I promise you."

There was doubt mixed in with the pain on her beautiful round face, but she nodded in agreement when we planned a meeting with everyone in our magic group. She burrowed deeper between me and Merry, like she was sucking up all the comfort she could get. We let her, the three of switching our positions so we could huddle close on the couch. All of us had been marked by magic in some way, good or bad. Two of us, it seemed, were now made up of magic.

FIVE

TO SAY MY WORRY over Mia ratcheted up would be a massive understatement. She'd been off all summer, and to know exactly why she was off didn't help calm my nerves. What did calm me, slightly, was the fact Harley, Gareth, and Ny agreed to a meet—not only a meet but to help my sister without blowing their lids at what she'd done. Mia didn't need stress or guilt now. She already had enough she'd created herself. She needed answers, and if people didn't have immediate answers, she needed a plan to move forward. Get the help she needed to stop whatever it was she had in her head from taking over more and more of her.

The bright spot, and hopeful stress reliever for me, was my group date with Gareth and Ny. It gave me a chance to let go of my worry and have fun. We'd have to see how much fun, and what variety of fun, would be had. Regardless, some type of fun would be had, damnit.

At the least, we'd eat good food. Gareth had called to run his dinner plans by me, and I'd approved. We were meeting at an old-school steakhouse, one of the longest-running restaurants in Columbus. I'd only been twice, and both times had been memorable. The place was like something out of a Rat Pack movie, all dark-wood paneling, dimmed lamp light, white table-cloths over solid oak tables, and comfy leather chairs. It was a 1950s-style joint still thriving in the twenty-first century. Plus there were the steaks, expertly broiled and topped with an onion ring, no matter the cut or style. A real treat, for sure.

To mark the occasion—great food with two guys I cared about and had sex with and might have sex with together—I dolled myself up. The atmosphere of the place called for sexy-classy, so I went a bit Marilyn Monroe in my garb, without the blonde hair, of course. I even bought a new dress, a white bodycon number with rouching throughout the bodice. It hit a few inches below my ample thighs and hoisted my breasts up to the gods. I took the time to curl my dark hair so it cascaded around me in soft waves. My makeup was smoky-eyes paired with a red lip. I was looking good, good enough I put a little extra strut in my walk as I entered the restaurant on the silver strappy high-heeled sandals, which perfectly matched my tiny, silver-sparkling clutch.

As soon as I passed the huge black doors and stepped into the bar area of the restaurant, my eyes landed on the guys standing together. Gareth's hair wasn't tied back but was pushed behind his ears so his face still looked beautifully open. He leaned back, one arm propped up on the bar while the other dangled down his side, a beer bottle hanging from the end of his long, strong hand. He wore a plain white button up, crisp and rigid, but the sleeves were rolled up so his large, tattooed forearms were highlighted. He also wore light-gray slacks and big black boots—his usual footwear. His choices felt vaguely familiar, and it struck me suddenly that he looked like an odd, opposite mirror of Harley. A laugh bubbled up at the thought of Gareth going to her to get styling tips. With Gareth's stoic calm and Harley's no-nonsense attitude she so quickly turned to snark, I'd have liked to witness the conversation if it had happened.

Ny leaned beside Gareth, his head tilted slightly toward the man as if he were telling some secret, his back to the bar and his lean supported by his elbows being propped up along its edge. He didn't straighten when he saw me, but the slow blink he gave, so like a cat happy to see a human they liked, was reaction enough from him. He wore dress pants, a matching vest, and a matching charcoal-gray button-up shirt beneath. It was the first time I'd seen him out of his leather jacket, and he looked damn good. When I got closer, I noticed the crisscrossing blacks and grays in an almost imperceptible plaid pattern to his pants and vest. Each garment hugged his leanly muscled form tightly, showing it to its best advantage.

"I thought I went all out, but this…" I said, gesturing with my clutch in an up-and-down motion at the two men who stepped up to me.

"We pale in comparison to your glow tonight, lovely," Ny purred as he took my hand and kissed the back in greeting.

Gareth said nothing at first, letting his hungry eyes tell what they wanted until he took me in a quick, tight hug and whispered, "You look delicious, Randy." The words, and the feel of them hot and hard in my ear, made me flush.

I stepped back to survey the place and asked, "Were you waiting on me or the table?"

"The table," Gareth answered, twisting to reach for a glass on the bar. He handed it to me and I sniffed, the smell of citrus and bourbon telling me he knew to order me an Old Fashioned.

"Please. Sit," Ny said, gesturing at a stool in between the spots they had occupied at the bar.

"Oh, I will. These shoes aren't made for standing around," I said, half joking. With all honesty, those things were cute as hell but they also hurt like hell if I stood around in them too long.

"Well worth the sacrifice, I'm sure," Ny said with gruff heat as he helped me up onto the stool.

"For sure. They're pretty and pain-free if I'm sitting. Or lying."

"Randy," Gareth growled, moving closer so I felt his calm and his heat seep into my skin.

"Don't make promises, sweetling," Ny said, moving in closer on his side as well.

Promise and potential hovered in the air between us. I didn't speak, didn't push it further, but my heart fluttered at the ideas racing in my mind. Ideas I cooled only slightly with a long, burning sip of my drink.

WE HAD A FABULOUS meal. Partly because the food was so good. I had prime rib with a giant baked potato and enjoyed every bite of it. Partly because the flirting was cranked up to eleven. I sat between the men. Gareth's hazel eyes scraped across my skin, leaving a trailing of heat. Occasionally he reached out and squeezed my hand when something witty or flirty I said made him chuckle, his eyes crinkling and head partially thrown back. He was calming, sure. Like he always was. Didn't mean the lust didn't sizzle between us like it always did. Only difference was Ny added to the mix.

The Prince, as Harley had recently reminded me, lounged in his chair like one. It was how I imagined someone in Versailles would sit. Not just the insolent lean, but the always-feline cast to his look and general air. He was the big cat who looked out at the world as if it were his to do with as he wished. Like any lion or tiger or panther in the wild, he wasn't exactly wrong.

There was a certain confidence he exuded from knowing, without doubt, his place in the world he inhabited, especially if the place was on high. He was an apex predator in this world, even without his power at 100 percent.

Except when he turned toward me. The flippancy was a joke between us on occasion, but his eyes heated just like Gareth's, and his odd chivalry was always on display. When he touched me, a soft stroke of my voluminous black curls or a reach up to brush across my shoulders or a squeeze of my knee under the table when he laughed at a joke I or Gareth made, my skin sizzled with power and magic. DD was in its happy place, bouncing up and down, shaking with joy as it hovered a little closer to Ny than maybe it should have. I couldn't say my heart didn't melt a smidge when, at one point during dinner, as Ny had raised his glass for a drink, he'd steered his hand close enough to DD to give it an affectionate nudge with a knuckle. DD had been ecstatic. I understood Gareth's hesitancy on one level, but Ny's acknowledgment and comfort with DD was a different type of comfort for me.

We ate, we joked, and we talked about hiking trails in Hocking Hills—a pastime Gareth enjoyed—and my love of a good dance party, which brought me to a question I'd never really asked. "How did you show up at Heatwave?"

Ny cocked his head, as if thinking about how he would give his answer before he spoke. "I was thrust from my power, ripped from my usual trajectory, and all I knew was I was in Columbus, in a time before you, but needed to get to you. I was weak, but not so weak I couldn't contain and marshal the power others gave off. A lovely couple invited me into their home and I used their discarded energy to project to you."

"You're talking sex magic, right?"

"Yes, sweetling. I harnessed the energy they threw off during sex, something I learned to do with humans long ago."

"It was the three of you then? All together? It allowed you to do major magic?" I didn't exactly need a reason to be with both Gareth and Ny at the same time, but the sex magic conversation was important. However we joined, being clear about expectations in all things physical and magical would be important.

"They were a beautiful couple who cared for each other a great deal, which allowed for the creation of fairly potent magic—for the average human. If you're asking what would be produced by us, it would be something different and even more powerful."

Gareth cleared his throat and adjusted in his seat. I doubted the conversation was making him physically uncomfortable, what with the way he bit his lip and his eyes blazed, so I was sure a different, sweeter sort of discomfort was taking over. Mostly I was sure because my own core was clenching at the thought. He reached across the table, taking my hand in his big, tattooed one, and said in a gruff voice, "There will be magic and power, like there is when we are separate. Most definitely. Don't let the idea sway you if you don't wish to explore with both of us for your own pleasure."

"Quite right," Ny said. "We all care for each other in our own way, but you are our nexus of care, Randy. Our feelings for you are deep and vast as the night. As much as we may wish to express our adoration together, and possibly see what the three of us produce, it is not something we would do at the risk of our connection with you. We only move forward with your surety, and only at your pace."

"There's a lot going on, but we've been busy bees for the past several months." I wanted to be clear with them. "I can't say the exploration of magic isn't a big incentive, especially if it allows for things like astral projection. There's a lot of ways this sort of magical power might come in handy, but really, I just want you both. It feels right to have you both."

Ny swirled his hand in the air, and our waiter materialized as if summoned. Maybe Ny did summon him, I don't know. All I knew in that moment was the hunger on his face and the clutch of Gareth's warm hand in my own. "We'll need the check, please."

"Can I offer you any dessert?"

Gareth's deep voice said in a low boom, "No need. We have dessert covered."

Six

GARETH WASN'T ONLY USING innuendo. I did have a special dessert prepared back at my place—napoleons piled high with flaky, buttery puff pastry, vanilla pastry cream, and tiger-striped chocolate and vanilla glaze crowning it. The dessert took time and effort. I didn't make them for my café but still loved to indulge in them every now and again. Seemed fitting for me and my guys and our first official group date.

Ny made his way back to my place through his usual shadowy means. I was going to take an Uber, but Gareth asked me to ride with him on his motorcycle. When I claimed my dress was too tight and short and heels too high, he stared at my legs and thighs in silence for a full thirty seconds, like his brain was going haywire at the thought of them wrapped around him on his bike. He then stalked forward, making me back-pedal until my butt hit the wall beside the door to the restaurant.

"Ride with me," he said, his voice and the cage of his arms, the feel of his hot body, causing a shiver to run riot through my body.

All I could do was nod. He gave a smile full of dark satisfaction and tugged my hand until I was following him out the door and onto his bike, after tucking my tiny clutch under his seat.

No lie, the vibrations and the warmth of Gareth's back against my nearly exposed core had me achy and on edge by the time we pulled into my back lot.

Ny stood waiting outside for us, even though he could have easily made his way into my apartment. Always so civil and courteous, to me at least. The spark of danger, the darkness swirling in his eyes, was a clear warning to others and a secret thrill for me. Ny gave me space and time in so many real and metaphorical ways, but I had no illusions about him behaving the same with others. He was not bad, as both Harley and Mia had explained in the abstract before I'd even met him officially. He simply was an Outer God who did as he wished, and for some unfathomable reason, the way he acted screamed what he wished for most in this realm, at this time, was to please me. I didn't understand it, likely couldn't because I didn't see time and space the same and had never known the Book of Knowing that made him oh-so certain about me and the idea of us. I also didn't look a gift god in the mouth. Or, more aptly, I didn't mind having the gift of an Outer God's mouth when it was so focused on me in a sexy, good-times-will-be-had-by-all kind of way.

Ny was at the motorcycle before I'd peeled the helmet from my head. He took it from me with one hand as he extended the other, offering to help me off the machine. My legs were a little wobbly, from my heels and the ride and the sensations amping me up. Ny took note of it. His face, the ancient Pharoah made flesh in all its regal glory, twitched in a feline gesture of scenting, which was followed by a slow smile.

"Sweetling," he purred as he pulled me off balance so I fell against his chest. "What have you been thinking about while hugged so tightly to our dear Gareth?"

"Our dear Gareth" sounded out of place from him, though not fully. Not really. Not after I rolled it around in my mind. He was our dear Gareth in a way. The same way Ny was our sweet Prince and I was their sweetling.

I didn't answer the question. Couldn't in all honesty, not unless I wanted to rev all three of us up out in the open parking lot. It was a conversation for my apartment. Instead, I pulled away and led the guys, with a little extra shimmy of my hips, up into my home.

Once there, I motioned for them to lounge as I prepped the dessert. I served it on pretty silver dessert plates I only busted out on special occasions. What was likely happening tonight, given the throbbing lust in my blood, definitely qualified as a special occasion.

There were no words, as if all three of us worried about breaking a spell of lust and longing we'd conjured together. We ate some of the napoleons, the guys giving me soft grunts of enjoyment to mark how much they liked it. We didn't finish them though. Any other time I might have considered it a waste, but not this night.

As I took a hearty bite of pastry and cream, my fork slipped too close to the corner of my mouth. Swallowing quickly, I gave an embarrassed giggle and muttered, "My bad," as I reached for a napkin to wipe the smear of pastry cream on my lips. Ny was there in a flash, one second across from me at the dining table and the next kneeling by my side, his hand stopping the napkin.

"Allow me?" he asked, his voice so low I felt it more than I heard it.

I nodded, lost in his nighttime eyes as he moved closer, licked his deliciously scratchy tongue across my lips, and lapped up the cream there.

I gasped. I couldn't help it. It didn't make it far in the room, however, before it was drowned out by the deep groan of appreciation from Gareth, who let his own fork clamor to his plate. I turned my head slightly, letting Ny continue to lick and suck down my jaw, down my neck, where he finally stopped to pay special attention to the sensitive crease where my neck met my shoulder.

I parted my lips—to pant or plead, I didn't know. Nothing came. I was trapped between the hot, scratchy licks of Ny's tongue and the nearly feral look in Gareth's eyes. Yet it wasn't possession or sadness or dominating will I saw in his hazel gaze. It was need and desire and encouragement. His chest rose and fell in jerking motions, as if every breath was a struggle. He finally ground out, "How do you feel, Randy?"

A moan ripped up my throat and I tipped my head back, giving Ny more access to my chest, where he peppered kisses across the top of my dress, the swell of my breasts.

He lifted his lips from me long enough to say with his imperious, cool tone of his, "I believe he'd like actual words, lovely."

I huffed a semi-laugh and answered, "I'll get on that when I can think again."

Ny responded with his own satisfied masculine chuckle. I wanted to joke, to poke and give snark, but before I could reply, he slipped the top of my dress down, exposing my breasts to the air before he clamped a hard nipple between his teeth and gave a powerful suck.

There were no more words from me then, only moans and squirms in my seat for a solid few minutes.

"Goddamn," Gareth said.

Ny popped off my nipple to give Gareth a wink from across my half-naked body. "I'm not damning anyone tonight."

The joke broke the mood slightly, enough to have me pushing Ny away. He shot up to his feet instantaneously, worry clear in the deep crease of his brow. "Are you okay, sweetling? Did I progress too quickly?"

I shook my head and took the time to slowly rise from my chair and push it away from the table, to give me room for what I wanted to do. "Nope," I said with a pop. I hooked my hands in his vest hem and pulled him close, planting soft kisses on his face as I unbuttoned and removed the vest, flinging it and, eventually, his shirt to the floor. My hands roamed his warm, brown chest, toying lightly with the line of black hair leading into his plaid pants.

"I want a taste too," I said, sinking to my knees and freeing his hard length from behind his zipper.

Ny hissed in true cat fashion as I palmed his erection, stroking up and down a moment to spread the beads of moisture at his tip down the rest of him. I turned to look at Gareth, locked in a hungry stare behind me, and gave my own wink right before I focused back on my treat and took Ny into my mouth.

"Oh, fuck. So good, sweetling," Ny said, adjusting his stance slightly so he could remain upright and un-wavering under my ministrations. I licked and sucked, taking him deep into my mouth, to the very back of my throat, before pulling off and starting over again.

I wiggled my ass at Gareth as I did, which he took as an invitation. Slowly, so I could stop him if I wanted, he pushed the bottom hem of my dress up, over my hips and ass, until the whole thing, top and bottom, was bunched around my gently swaying belly. His large hands, warm and soothing, roamed over my dimpled ass in my white lace cheeky panties. Eventually he dipped down and stroked across my soaked core over my panties, and I couldn't stifle the jolt of my body or the deep moan in my throat at the contact.

"Shit. Do it again," Ny said as he ran his hands through my thick black hair. He wasn't controlling exactly, more like guiding. I looked up at him, his neck straining in need and desire, and I felt like the most powerful being on this planet, the one person who seemed designed to bring this Outer God to his knees.

I doubled my efforts, wanting to give Ny a spectacular orgasm and have Gareth witness all of it. Gareth did watch, I was sure, but he also played with my body, slipping under my panties to rub against my clit as he talked to me and Ny.

"You like the taste of him, Randy? The feel of him in your mouth while I play with your soaking pussy?"

It was the dirtiest of talk and I reveled in it, moaning around Ny and pushing back against Gareth's hand to get more pressure.

"How's her mouth feel, Ny?" he asked from behind me.

"It feels glorious. Truly divine."

"Good," Gareth growled, bending down to lie across my back, bring his face closer to my ear, closer to where Ny was now starting to thrust into my mouth in earnest. "You going to let me fuck you after he comes in your mouth?"

All I could do was moan and wiggle my agreement, because Ny was a thing possessed. I looked up and saw him staring with his dark nebulous eyes, the eyes of power he had whenever we had sex. They practically glowed black as he roared a warning before he spent deep down my throat.

The room shimmered with magic, black and starry and swirling in shadow as per usual, though it was not fully complete. That came only when both of us came.

Ny pulled himself from my mouth then bent to gently pull me up from my knees and give me a deep, searing kiss. He smiled sharply as he looked behind at Gareth before he pressed me into the now-naked blond man. Gareth grabbed hold and gave me his own searing kiss before he wrenched himself away and said, "I can't wait."

I nodded, fully understanding the feeling, as I was dripping with need and ready to let go. I turned to the table and bent forward, sticking my butt in the air and giving it a shimmy so my thighs and ass jiggled in clear invitation. I heard Gareth growl, then the rip of a foiled condom wrapper.

"Ready?" he asked, pausing his own drive to move to check with me.

I pushed against him, greedy and more than ready, and breathed out, "Yes," a millisecond before he slammed home, thrusting himself inside me in one forceful, swift motion. I screamed at the feeling of fullness, of rightness, and stretched my arms out in front of me on the table as my back arched so hard my breasts lifted off the surface. Then Ny was there, taking my hands, holding me tight and taut, as Gareth plowed into me.

He gave a few experimental strokes, but we'd been together enough at this point for him to know how to maneuver himself inside me for maximum effect. Within moments, he was nudging the spot behind my clit with each stroke in and out, his head bumping it over and over again until I was making nearly incoherent cries of "yes" and "more" and "just like that."

Ny let go of one of my arms to cup my face, force my eyes onto him, as he purred, "He fucks you so well, lovely."

"Yes. Yes. Yes… He does," I cried out, my words punctuated with grunts from behind.

Gareth gripped my hips tighter, pulling my body up slightly off the table to angle me more sharply. It made each thrust sweet torture, until I was ready. All I could do was moan, then scream, as my orgasm tore through me, throwing magic out into the dark swirl already present, adding depth to the shadows there.

Gareth's strokes stuttered, then intensified, and he came on a deep, dark moan, folding himself down on top of me as he jerked with release inside my body. I noticed something new, something lighter, in the usual starry magic swirl Ny and I made. A bit of moss-green light was infusing the darkness. The piece Gareth added.

"Yes, sweetling. It's all of us now," Ny said, standing to slip something from his pants pocket.

Gareth had straightened, and he brought me up off the table in a warm, comforting hug of a grip, setting me on slightly shaking feet. He kissed my cheek gently, fully engulfed me in his tattooed arms from behind, and rested his chin on my shoulder. "Our magic is beautiful," he said, his voice slightly hoarse.

"Yep." I watched Ny open an old-timey-looking pocket watch but was too relaxed and blissed out post orgasm to ask questions.

"We created this excess, but I do believe now is not the time to truly experiment with it. I think we require rest first."

In full agreement, more than a little tired after good food and fabulous sex, I watched silently as he waved his hand in some pattern and the magic swirled down, down, down, into the face of the darkly glowing watch.

Ny snapped it shut and said, "There. Tucked away tight. Now, for rest." He grabbed one of my hands and led me to my own bedroom, which I allowed because I was tired. Tired enough to strip down and lie between Gareth and Ny without any talk or worry. I wore only a satisfied smile as I lay between my guys and felt the calm of Gareth at my front and the zap of Ny's electric magic at my back from head to toe. I snuggled down and hoped for better dreams as I drifted off to sleep.

SEVEN

I KISSED BOTH MY guys long and hard before they left the next morning. Gareth had to get to the library for work way too early, so he didn't linger long and didn't say much. When I offered my mouth, he pulled me from bed and held me tight to his chest, making me breathless. He stroked my cheek with what felt like true affection and whispered, "Bye," in his gruff voice before sauntering out of my apartment.

Because I'd crawled out of bed to say good-bye to the big guy, I grudgingly decided to stay awake and get an early start. There were two big wedding cupcake orders on for the weekend, so it'd be good to get to my kitchen earlier than usual.

When I stepped from my bathroom, teeth and hair brushed and cold water splashed on my face for an extra pick-me-up, Ny was leaning against the door-jamb of my bedroom, arms crossed over his bare chest, unbuttoned plaid dress pants slung low, and a smirk on his face.

"Sweetling," he purred. His voice, both soft and rough, skidded across my skin, reminding me of the scratchiness of his delicious tongue. My skin pebbled at the memory, and so did my nipples, something Ny didn't miss as his gaze darted up and down my body and his chest emitted a low rumble.

"None of that, you," I said, playfully shoving him. Somehow the Outer God hadn't expected it. He wobbled a bit and had to take a step back on his foot and straighten his torso to maintain his balance. It was odd enough I stopped and said, "You good?"

He blinked a few times, the dark slash of his brows creased and bunched in the middle of his forehead before he shook it off and threw me a wide smile. "Yes, lovely. I am good. Although, I am hungry."

"For breakfast, I hope, because food's all you're getting from me this morning. I have things to do."

He chuckled, hands up in supplication. "Breakfast would be marvelous."

Ny sat at the kitchen bar, and I pulled out the muffins and iced coffee I'd ferreted away from the café the day before. We sat in easy silence for a time, munching away without much thought about anything in particular. At least, I had little thought. It was still early for me, so my brain might have been lagging some.

When I became less dazed, I stood and stretched tall, trying to pull out the remaining sleepiness. I turned toward Ny, who eyed me with an easy smile. "Sore?" he asked.

"Nope. We didn't do anything too straining last night."

In a flash, he was up and I was in his arms. "We'll have to remedy that in the future," he whispered as his sharp nose tickled my ear. His lips started there and trickled down, leaving feathery kisses in their wake.

"Ny," I said, in a plea. To stop or go further was a toss-up for a second, but I managed to take a side. I squirmed in his arms and said, "Not now. I have baking to do."

He loosened his grip as he lifted his mouth from my body, and I felt the loss of both in my gut. "As you wish, sweetling." He disappeared in a blink and showed back up almost as quickly, buttoning up his dress shirt from last night. "I will leave you to your work."

"What's your plan for the day?" I asked, then realized I didn't know what Ny did with most of his days.

He fiddled with something in his trouser pocket before lifting out the pocket watch where he'd stored our excess sex magic from last night. "I'm off to explore."

"The magic?"

"No. New ways to hold it. I have a feeling storage may be an issue. I will contact Harley to ask if she knows of any possible solutions, and how we might acquire such a solution."

I nodded. I definitely wanted more of last night, and if the amount of magic we'd produced then was an indication of what we'd always produce when the three of us were together, we most definitely needed more storage. Harley was the occult-ish wheeler and dealer.

If anyone knew of some object we could get to help, it'd be her.

"Sounds like a plan," I said, pulling him into me to give my own kisses, as deep and long as I'd kissed Gareth earlier. Needed to be equal and all that. "I'm off to shower and bake."

Ny tilted his head and quipped, "Sure you don't require company in your shower?"

I laughed and said, "No. I can manage on my own, thank you very much." I forced him to turn around, swatted his firm and luscious butt playfully, and said, "Now get."

He threw an amused and slightly arrogant look over his shoulder and sauntered toward my door. "Until later, sweetling." He didn't use the door. Instead, he stepped seamlessly into a slightly shadowed corner and was gone.

I gave him a wave and a wink, putting my own arrogant swagger in place, then moved to the bathroom as soon as the door closed behind him. A cold shower might've been good, but I liked my showers long and as hot as Satan's tears, especially early in the morning, so hot it was.

I WAS DRESSED IN leggings and a tee, toweling my hair and trying to decide if I wanted to waste time drying it or let it go, as I'd put it up in a messy bun either way, when I heard a jangle of keys against my lock. I poked my head out of the bathroom to see Mia shuffle into the apartment.

"What up?" I asked.

"Not much. Light day today. Thought I'd see what you're up to."

Deciding then to put my hair up without blow drying and call it a day, I moved from the bathroom into the open space of my apartment as I twisted a scrunchy around the wet, black mass I'd piled at the top of my head. "Thought you'd grab some breakfast, more like." I hoped my teasing landed. We'd always had a banter-y type relationship, more so than Merry and me, and I'd missed it over the past few months. All the shit swirling around Mia, namely the completion and invasion of that damn book, made her not her usual self, including not being open to snarky banter.

She snorted, a minimal sign of her attitude but a positive sign, which gave me hope. I pulled the iced coffee back out and handed Mia a zucchini muffin. "Here you go. Packed with veggies and sweetness. All a growing girl needs."

"I'm grown enough, thanks."

It was my turn to snort. "Okay five-foot-nothing. Whatever you say."

She didn't bite back, but I was happy we'd had a glimmer of the old Mia and Randy. I moved to sit beside her at the bar while she ate, and I didn't give her silence and space like I had Ny.

"How're you feeling?" I didn't think I needed to explain the question. We'd texted a little back and forth, all the Carter sisters, since our Mia intervention two nights ago. She'd know what I meant.

"Same, but not really? It's hard to explain. The voice is there, but it's not a secret anymore so it feels less heavy. There's been a weird pulse a few times. The book popped up on random screens in a way it hadn't before now, like it was calling out instead of waiting."

"Not a good sign, Mia."

"I know. Our big meeting is soon, so we can figure it all out together. Until then, I need to get some work done so I don't lose my condo."

I gave a harsh laugh. "Capitalism sure doesn't care about magic problems. Which is why I need to get down to the bakery too. Come on. We'll clear a space for you somewhere down there. Me, you, and Nate will all work together today."

I moved to grab my shoes from the bedroom and was slipping them on when I heard Mia call out, "Cool vest."

She was wearing Ny's vest when I came from the room, and it made me laugh. The dark, almost imperceptible plaid didn't quite fit over Mia's boobs, but it did fall down to almost her thighs. "That's Ny's," I said by way of explanation.

Mia looked down at it, a small frown on her face. "Really? I've never seen him in anything outside his goth leather-daddy look."

I might have blushed when I said, "We had a date last night. Me and Ny. And Gareth."

Mia's mouth dropped wide open. "Oh. My. God. Why didn't you say anything?" She whipped out her phone from her jeans pocket, her fingers flying across the screen as she muttered, "Merry needs to know this right now."

"Thanks for putting my dating life on blast, sis. Really appreciate it."

She stuffed her phone back in her pocket, threw her hands on her hips like the old Mia, and shouted, "I can't believe you didn't tell me! Or us. Whatever. You didn't say anything, and this is very juicy sister gossip, so you need to spill. Immediately."

The attitude, the stance, it all came back to past Mia. Instead of banter bubbling up, tears welled in my eyes. I rushed to her and gave her a fierce hug as a strangled laugh came up my throat. I'd been so worried, for so long, but the look of her now gave me real encouragement, and I wanted to cling to it—to the idea Mia would be okay and be herself again one day soon.

"Not now," I managed to say, wiping tears quickly before looking her up and down. "Later. We'll talk all about it with Merry."

"We better," she said with a small pout.

"Promise," I whispered before I held her at arm's length and wrinkled my nose. "You smell like Ny with this thing on," I said.

"What's Ny smell like?" she asked, sniffing her shoulder and the vest.

I couldn't describe it well, the way he smelled, because it was mixed up in so many other senses. "Like shadow and night, and wilderness, and maybe a little sweet spice, like cardamom."

Mia looked at me confused for a second, then simply shook her head. "Whatever. I like it."

"You look like a nerd girl trying to be a scene kid and failing at it."

The gasp of pure affront was refreshing, and I laughed, long and loud, before I hooked my arm in hers. "He might want it back," I said as we headed to my bakery kitchen.

"Finder's keepers. He can ask for it back if he gets upset about it or something." She pulled on the open vest, tugging it more firmly in place on her frame.

"You don't think it's weird?"

"What would be weird?"

"You know, you wearing cast-off clothes of my..." I let the sentence fall. Ny and I weren't defined, by my own doing mostly.

"Oh, you want to say something, Randy? Stake some claim?" Mia asked, in a voice I hadn't heard from her in a while, her sickly-sweet baby-sister voice she used to use when she teased. Which was what she was doing,

I realized. She was needling me to make some sort of declaration because she thought I should. Well, she'd wait a while longer for it.

"Never mind. Wear the stupid thing if you want to look like a reject from the Warped Tour à la 2007."

I cackled at my own joke as Mia followed me down the stairs, grumbling all the way, still clutching Ny's vest to herself out of pure stubbornness.

TWO HOURS LATER, I was deep in structure construction as a whole mess of cupcakes baked. Nate and Mia chatted occasionally while working on the other side of the kitchen. Deb came through the door separating the café and kitchen. "Got a minute?" she asked as I fiddled with some cardboard.

"Sure. What's up?"

"We need to talk about Yasmiin."

"What?" Yasmiin was one of my best employees. I couldn't think of what Deb might possibly need to talk to me about regarding her.

"Oh, no, no, no," she said, catching my surprise. "Nothing bad. Don't worry. It's just... Things are getting even busier, and we need more help. Really, I need more help. And Yasmiin knows everything about the front of this place. Maybe we could give her more responsibility?"

I tilted my head in thought. I sure as hell wasn't helping out much beyond baking, even with the magic business slowing down. I worked better in the kitchen than in the café, though I took register shifts when I was needed there. To be honest, Deb was keeping it all afloat, with the help of Nate and Yasmiin already. It would make sense to give all of them more responsibility, level out the load so Deb wasn't drowning in order to keep my business afloat.

"Let me talk to Merry," I said. From what I knew of current numbers, I could afford to give both Yasmiin and Nate raises. I understood what I had now was different than what I could expect in the future. Merry was the one with the projections and figures in her accounting work, so I needed to sit with her and go over the numbers before I could say for certain what could or couldn't happen.

Deb nodded, knowing how much Merry helped with these things, and moved up to look at what I was doing. "Are you... building a football?"

"Go Bucks," I said with more than a little sarcasm. "It's for the groom's cake order this weekend. They wanted a platform shaped like a multi-tiered football to house all the cupcakes."

Deb laughed. "People are weird."

I agreed. As I stared at the thing, trying to figure out what type of pipes I'd need to keep the whole thing up, DD started frantically jumping at my side, as if to get my attention. I quirked my head, trying to calm it down without looking like a crazy person in front of Deb, who couldn't see the small mass of shadow now thrashing at my side. It zipped forward, in front of my eyes, then back to my side. That was when I noticed something along the wall behind the cardboard. It looked like a small crack. Only, it didn't stay small. It widened more and more, spidering out as I watched. Then, thick shadows trailed out, becoming more and more solid, turning into the tentacled shadows from my dreams—the same thick, oozing tentacles of shadows from the witch house. The crack widened, growing rapidly, and I had just enough time to throw up DD as a shield before Deb cried out in alarm as the whole wall buckled outward, a bubble bursting into a mass of rubble, flinging me and Deb into the air.

EIGHT

THE BLAST THROUGH THE air hurt like hell–both in the impact of bits of drywall and concrete and whatever other building materials were flung out and the hard drop right on my ass and back—but it didn't faze me for long. I saw stars, and definitely not the fun-times-with-Ny type of stars. The streak of floating flashes blinked across my vision, and the breath was knocked out of me from the good wallop I'd received. I could still see, so I watched in growing horror as the tentacled dark leaked out more and more, and Wilbur stepped from the gaping hole now marring my beautiful kitchen.

His body moved in slo-mo as first, as if he was moving toward us against a strong current. A crackle of magic scorched the air. The atmosphere of the kitchen felt like it dropped and gained pressure in a millisecond, making my ears pop painfully, and I had to slap my hands against them to try to get them unstuck. Then he was there, right in front of us, though he still looked disjointed and out of place in the new hole in my kitchen wall.

He didn't have a speck of dust on him from the explosion he'd caused, but he still looked and felt dirty. Wrong. A thing not supposed to be here. Not only in Warm Regards, but here, on this plane, at this time. He was a step outside what was supposed to be and moved like it. His motions were jerky and forced until a whip crack of magic sizzled in the air, and his form flickered a moment before he became solid and fixed in place and time. He wasn't totally in our time, because his clothes were old-fashioned and not in a quirky hipster way. A wide-brimmed black hat was perched on his head. He wore a vest-and-suit combo, but unlike Ny last night, it did nothing to make him look attractive. It was stern, the outfit of an old-timey preacher about to rail against some sin or another with threats of fire and brimstone. Only Wilbur was the fire and brimstone come to call.

His greasy hair and wiry goatee trembled as he stepped with too much impact, as if he landed in the room from a great distance rather than suddenly appearing out of nowhere. His black dress shoes, polished to a high shine, took the impact oddly, making his foot appear to wobble and shuffle at an inhuman angle. I could see the foot weirdness clearly as my face rested on the floor, staring up from ground level.

A leer down at me broke my daze, and I struggled up to my hands in knees, gritting through residual pain from my impact. I looked back, frantic to find Mia, who I saw was huddled across the room with Nate, both staring in horror at the evil shit coming out of the new hole in my wall.

It was a look that cost, however. Cost dearly. I turned in time to see Wilbur scooping a trembling Deb off the floor, her mouth opening and closing in pain or shock of the utter absurdity the situation, given she knew nothing of magic or shadows or evil, half-human goat-looking men. He dragged her up his body as I scrambled forward on hands and knees, trying to reach her. He sneered in her face, spit out the word "human" like a slur, and with one bony hand—strengthened with whatever magic he held—he reached up, stroked her cheek, then twisted her head around until it made a sickening crack and hung limp on her body.

I'd screamed. I thought. I knew Mia screamed, her cry a shot in the shard of soul still in my body as tears blurred my vision again. I heard Nate shout, registered something like a scrambling sound, and took another desperate look back. Mia was clinging to him, trying to get him down, to not charge toward the thing—maybe it had once been a man—who'd flung my friend to the ground like she were a crumbling scarecrow after Halloween.

Black overtook my vision, the same searing black rage I'd used to help me and my sisters escape Starry Wisdom. Except, I knew more now about magic and my own power. I seethed, burned, and twisted a hand out to grab those tentacles of darkness I feared in my dreams, the ones I'd used only once before in a previous fight. My kitchen had turned into a surreal place, where my friend could be killed right in front of me and I'd be too out of it or slow to do a damn thing to help her.

DD wavered but stayed strong, and I flung it behind me, partly to protect it from what was coming my way, but mostly to protect Mia and Nate, who huddled behind me. I heard Nate yell my name, which Mia shushed, as I called those darker shadows to my command to take Wilbur. To squeeze whatever life there was right the hell out of him.

They did my bidding, despite Wilbur's curses and words and flinging of magic. He struggled in the binds as they grew, slithering up from his feet to encircle his whole body. I staggered to my feet, pouring power into the tentacle things, pouring my rage and hurt and will, every drop I could give, until I reached some type of limit. Some hard stop screeched inside and made my control sputter and jerk, like a car engine dying.

Shaking, I dropped to my knees and watched Wilbur writhe for a moment before he pulsed with an eerie yellow light and the shadows unfurled, then receded back, back, back, until they disappeared behind the darkness lurking at the center of the hole in the wall.

He walked up, crouched to look at me kneeling, and gave a toothy grin. "Miranda. A pleasure to see you again," he said, as he placed a grimy, bony hand on my chest and blasted some yellowish light out, knocking me back to the ground. Pinning me to the ground.

He stood, looking far too smug, as I thrashed under the weight of the light. I screamed, incoherent rage and sadness making words impossible for a moment. Wilbur enjoyed it all, content to watch me struggle, physically and emotionally, as he stood tall above me.

Finally, I was able to grit out, "What the fuck do you want from me?"

He chuckled. "Silly human woman. I don't want anything from *you*," he said, before slowly moving his gaze to the back, to where my sister and Nate still crowded together behind DD.

"No!" I screamed, flinging whatever I had out. DD came to my call, zipping to me and forming my spear, which I used to bash into the light holding me down. Sparks flew out with each impact, and I felt shudders and starts. It would work. But not in time. Never in time.

Wilbur strolled toward my sister. Toward Mia. The person I knew he wanted because he'd told me that shit before, and I'd been too blinded by my own magic issues and lulled by peace to see this coming. Mia had told us everything, had even said the book was talking to her in specifics. Whatever the Necronomicon was or could do, Wilbur wanted it desperately. As it was a part of Mia, he needed her. Would take her.

Nate surged up to run at the man, in vengeance or protection or a little bit of both, I couldn't rightly say. Wilbur swatted him back like a fly, a backhand straight to the face like he'd given me the first time we'd met. Nate went flying and landed hard against one of the prep tables before sliding down to the floor. Wilbur cocked his head, looking over Nate with less than disdain.

"Not only human," he muttered, then moved forward, dismissing Nate as something not of his concern but apparently worthy enough to live. Unlike Deb. Poor Deb, who I could see lying on the floor as I hacked into the light, lying still—now forever still and motionless—with her head and limbs and torso crumpled at odd angles.

"Mia Carter," Wilbur said as he looked down at my kneeling sister. "Come with me."

Fear shone in her eyes, but so did spunk and spark, the mark of all of us Carter sisters. "Don't think so, fuckhead," she yelled as she surged up and punched him right between the legs.

Guess magical Wilbur hadn't thought to protect his balls. He wheezed out a cry and fell to his knees. It gave Mia time to scramble up and look around, between me and Nate.

"Run!" I yelled desperately. "Get to Harley's. Now!" Harley could protect her, plus her place was the safest bet with all those wards and spells lining her condo.

Mia skidded to a stop and dropped to her knees, hovering above me, tears in her eyes. "I can't leave you," she said on a pant of breath as she struggled with the light bearing down on me, trying to get me free so I could get out too.

"Don't worry about me. Get out now!" I screamed in her face, willing her gone. I willed it so much, part of DD ballooned outward in a quick burst of power, over with before it even really began, but just enough to move her five or six feet across the floor. She moved to right in front of the giant hole Wilbur was now stomping toward. He grabbed my sister by her pixie cut so hard, I could see the skin of her head pulled taut from the force of it.

I couldn't find words, I simply screamed and cried, flung out my spear in a last-ditch attempt to stop him. Wilbur batted it aside and laughed, turning to me when he had one foot in the gaping hole. "Until me meet again, Miranda Carter," he said, and with a snide approximation of a smile, he pushed through whatever magic separated time and space within the hole he'd blown in my wall, entered whatever plane was back there, and dragged my kicking and screaming baby sister behind him as he went.

Nine

I WAS SCREAMING; RAGE and pain and a feral need to get out, out, out from under the sickly yellow glow pinning me to my kitchen floor poured out of me as a harsh sound. Nate was at the wall—past the crumpled drywall, where the gaping hole into whatever other plane Wilbur had crawled out from had once been—banging on what appeared to be solid brick and pipes. He skidded to me after a few beats, yelling frantically, which made me hear him over my own shrill voice.

"Randy. RANDY! Calm down, girl. I need you to talk to me and not just scream. I need to know you're physically okay."

I stopped screaming for a moment and swallowed, jagged stones tearing down my throat. When I breathed in and out, trying to draw on the focus Harley had taught me, I could begin to logically evaluate. I was stuck by this magic, Nate needed to know some things, and Mia was gone. The last part made a sob rip up my throat, tearing into the pain there, leaving more in its wake.

"Yes," I managed to say, after the wounded noise left me. It wasn't physical pain after all. It was a missing chunk of my soul. "I'm okay. But I need Ny. Or Harley. One of the two. Now."

"Randy, as much as I hate to say it for a variety of reasons, we need the cops."

"No. No cops." But as soon as the words were out of my mouth, a loud pop sounded, the atmosphere of the place shifting back into place, and pain hit my ears again. Nate winced as if he felt it too, and the door the café part of the kitchen swung open. Micah, the counter employee on duty, was running back, as if the rumble of an explosion had just sounded and not long minutes before. He skidded to a halt, taking in the jagged wall first, then me on the floor, and Nate hovering over me. Finally, Deb. Dead. Lying by the broken wall. A loud yelp of surprise and distress tore from his throat.

More cries of alarm from the café followed confusion falling all over the place, as the customers out front shouted questions because of the harsh cries they had heard in the back. Micah was crying over Deb, and Nate was torn between trying to care for his two living co-workers and his one dead friend. I wanted to cry, crawl in a dark hole somewhere and cry for days and days over what had just gone down, but I didn't have the luxury of that. Action was required, and I was the only one here who knew what was going on. I needed backup so maybe I could get to a place where the tears were allowed to shut everything else down.

"Nate," I said, finding some way to push through the pain and make decisions one step at a time. "Get all the customers out of the café. Call Harley and tell her to grab Merry and get here ASAP. Then, you and Micah sit out there and wait."

"No, I can't leave..."

"Nate," I clipped out, maybe a bit too harshly. "Get it done. Now. I'll be fine. Ny will come help."

He wanted to say more. I could see all the questions swimming in his worn-leather brown eyes, but he ran his fingers through his messy hair and gave a curt nod before jumping up and doing what I asked him to do.

I gathered DD to me, pulled it close, and offered it a moment of comfort to calm its jittering before I asked, "Can you get Ny for me?" I could call him, of course. My phone was around here somewhere. But I needed him now. DD jumped in reply, caressed my cheek, and blinked out for five seconds before popping back up again to skim my shoulder in a soft, reassuring gesture.

Then Ny was there, gathering me up off the floor in a lightning-quick pull of strong, warm arms. He'd forced the sickly yellow light away, swallowed it right up with a dark glow he projected from his hands. "Randy. Sweetling. What happened here?"

I gave myself a moment to cry. Buried my head in his ever-present leather jacket, the one I associated so much with Ny's scent—night and spices and wildness–and wept until I heard Merry's voice through the din of noise and knew I had to pull my shit together and get to work.

I WAS NUMB. MOSTLY. I'd come undone a bit when I heard Merry's wail when I told her Mia was gone. She'd wrapped her arms around me, shaking with her own anger and grief. My voice cracked with a broken sob as I shook in the comfort of her familiar hug. I hiccupped over and over again, "I'm sorry. I tried. I'm sorry. I tried."

Eventually, her soft hands in my hair calmed me enough for steel to wrap back up my spine, for my sadness to turn into my black rage which would inevitably become a need to do and fix.

I was vaguely aware of things happening around me I should have been focused on, but it was hard to think of the specifics when horrible scenarios including Mia and Wilbur kept creeping across my brain, making me itch to go, go, go and get her, damn everything else.

Ny and Harley talked in hushed voices in a corner. Gareth skidded in and wrapped me in his own calming hugs, hugs that made me feel a measure of comfort even if all I offered him at the time was silent, angry shaking.

Micah left. Nate eventually left after a long chat with Harley and Gareth. Cops came. So did an ambulance, to cart away Deb. Deb's body, which had lain broken on my kitchen floor for far too long.

I didn't know what Ny had done or said to the cops and EMTs. After he had gathered them all together, everyone official moved through the space quickly and asked no questions. Not really what I'd expect given the circumstances, but I was in no mood for questions or lies. All I could give those people were lies. I couldn't give them the truth: Deb was dead and Mia was taken, because of me and my magic.

Eventually, I found myself standing outside the bathroom in my apartment, Merry at my back. I looked down at myself, covered in debris, and a shower seemed like a good idea.

"Yeah. Uh. Yes. Okay. Guess I need to clean myself up a little," I croaked.

Merry squeezed my shoulders, gave me a tight hug, and said, "Take a quick shower. We'll be waiting."

I nodded and stripped down as soon as the door shut behind my sister. I stepped into icy-cold water, something to get me awake. Something to match the black rage bubbling in the center of my chest.

THE COLD SHOWER AND colder rage did the trick. I was clean and ready to take on whatever came our way, though what would come first was scarier: having to tell the gathered people in my apartment what happened below in detail.

Halting but firmly resolved to get it out as quickly as possible, I recounted it all to Merry, Harley, Ny, and Gareth, who sat gathered around at my dining room table. Merry was within arm's reach in the seat to my right, and she squeezed my hands tightly here and there whenever I hesitated or stumbled in my speech. Harley sat beside her, stiff in posture and eyeing me with intense focus while she managed to somehow also rub small circles across Merry's back. The comfort she gave tugged at my heart but made more guilt flair because I couldn't comfort Merry right now. Didn't deserve to, really.

Gareth and Ny stood in different poses. Gareth loomed close to my left, his calming vibes somewhat helpful as I told my tale, even if he didn't reach out to comfort me physically. Ny leaned on against the kitchen bar. It wasn't his usual cool, insolent, sexy lean. He looked tightly coiled, intense, and all his starry-eyed focus was on me as I spoke, as if he could watch what had happened unfold in front of him as each word tumbled from my mouth.

Once I was done, the question-and-answer period of the evening began.

Harley started, but to my surprise she turned to Ny instead of asking me anything. "How could Wilbur pull her through without the prep work?"

"Heavy magical power borrowed from somewhere else. The help of the shadows, possibly. However, the most important component was likely Mia's connection to the Necronomicon itself. It may have wanted to go with him, or been called through him to attend some other, more powerful being."

"We never..." Merry said, but tears threatened so she had to pause, gather herself with a deep breath, and start again after a few moments. "We were never able to discuss this book business with all of you like we wanted. Mia was scared, explained a little to us, but I honestly still don't get it."

Gareth jumped in with his information. "Randy told me of your conversation, and from what I gather, it seemed parts of the book fused with Mia in some way."

"She's not magical, so how could that even happen?" I asked.

"There are plenty of ways for the non-magical to force magic into themselves," Harley said.

"She wasn't a witch," I said between clenched teeth.

"I didn't say she was," Harley snapped back, not taking my shit. "Witches are one example, but only one. There are other forms. Some I know of, and likely many no one knows about."

Gareth touched my shoulder gently, and my head whipped around to him so quick, he flinched before he explained. "The Necronomicon hasn't been completed in centuries, and even when it was complete, no one discussed the process required for it to happen. It was an unexpected consequence, but not out of the realm of magical possibility."

"Mia and the book joined, in some odd way no one knew would happen, when she discovered the last bits of it. What does the book burrowing its way into Mia's mind actually mean for her?" Merry asked.

Ny joined the conversation. "The Necronomicon is an immensely powerful magical object. I'd never needed to use it, as I had the Book of Knowing, but others—powerful beings, old and new gods—could find what was in it very useful indeed. Just as they found my book useful."

"Are you suggesting whatever took your book is behind all this too?" Gareth asked.

"It all fits, doesn't it? Whoever it was has been attempting to amass power by any means necessary, here and within the Dreamlands. Wilbur is powerful, but he's just a pawn, as Macy was before him. It's a ladder, leading back to a singular, more powerful but not all-powerful being."

"Wait. How do you know this has anything to do with the Dreamlands?" I asked.

"Because those shadows, the tentacles you described from today, the ones we saw in the old house and you saw in your dreams? Those can only be found in the Dreamlands."

"And you never thought to mention this before?" Harley whispered, her tone lethal. Her exposed forearms crackled with what looked like purple lightening across her dark skin.

Ny eyed them as if fascinated, then shook himself. "It wasn't pertinent to explicitly explain. In the house, I told Randy the rip there fed directly into the Dreamlands."

He had, in fact, spoken of the Dreamlands, his home, when we'd first busted into the odd equation room with the shadowy rift. So much had happened after, the detail may have been lost in the shuffle of events.

"You think Mia's in the Dreamlands," Merry said, a declaration instead of a question. Ny nodded and she continued. "Is that a good or bad thing?"

The Outer God hesitated. "Both, I'm sorry to say. It is a dangerous place for humans, although some survive, even thrive there. It is a more dangerous place for a human who has possession of a thing power wants. We have two factors working in Mia's favor. First, Mia and the book are tied, and such binding magic is hard to break. This means she will need to remain alive if someone wishes to access all of the Necronomicon. Second, she carries a piece of me with her, a mark of me, which may protect her."

"Your vest," I said, glad I threw the small detail into my rendition of what had happened earlier in the day. It was a sliver of good in an ocean of bad shit, but I'd take any sliver I could hold on to just then.

"Exactly. A stroke of luck or kismet, as it were. She will carry the scent of me and my magic with her into my lands. Any one of my allies might find her and help her because of it."

"Okay. We need to hurry then."

"Hurry?" Harley asked.

"Hurry up and get to the Dreamlands to rescue her," I answered.

Ten

NO ONE SAID ANYTHING for a beat, then everyone started talking. Merry was against even the thought, Harley was muttering about stupid decisions, and Gareth was attempting to stay calm as he asked if I was certain, one hundred percent certain, that going to the Dreamlands was necessary. DD added its own unique commentary, hovering up to rest quietly on my shoulder as if it needed a rest to process what I'd said. I was about to shut all the chatter down when Ny beat me to it.

"Enough," he said, his voice talking on a cold and imperious note I'd never heard before, the tone of a Prince of the Dreamlands slithering out as we discussed his home. "Randy is correct. There is no other option. Mia requires our help. She cannot return on her own."

Everyone shut up real quick. I jumped into the silence. "This has a very real time limit. As in, we need to do it pronto before Mia's hurt too badly." I swallowed bile at the thought of all the things that could happen to my sister short of death. Ny had assured me she would not be killed. She was needed very much alive, in fact, if she was to be useful for whoever had had Wilbur take her in the first place. He hadn't reassured me as much as he probably thought. There was a whole lot of room for horrors between life and death, a whole lot that could break a person irrevocably. Permanent scars, physical or emotional, definitely hurt the living in a way death didn't touch, and I didn't want my little sister to have those marks on her body or soul. She needed our help, and she needed it ASAP.

"You said 'we' earlier," Harley stated, eyeing Ny then me. "Who do you mean by 'we' exactly? There may be a number of logistical issues there."

"Too true," Ny said before I could tell her we needed all hands on deck for this one. "The Dreamlands are not easily accessible to humans. Not impossible to reach, but not easily reached. There are, again, luckily, a number of things on our side in this. Randy's own magic makes her a likely candidate for easy transition from your plane to the plane of the Dreamlands without a massive expenditure of magic. We also happen to have a reserve of magic to help with any bumps along the way." Ny pulled the pocket watch from his jacket, and it crackled with the same dark energy we'd created what felt like eons before, but it had been last night. Damnit, things had turned on a dime.

Harley took in the watch, the thrum and spark of its power, then looked from Ny to Gareth to me. Nothing got past her, it seemed, but she didn't comment. Or joke. Or even smile. She gave a firm, stiff nod in approval of the excess of magic and made no remarks about how we got it. Always practical and to the point, she asked, "What can I do to help?"

"You and Merry can handle the issues here," Ny said softly, and I cursed out loud as tears gathered around my eyes yet again. I'd almost forgotten. The café, the employees. Deb. Mia needed help, yes, but so did people here and now. A person had died only hours ago, under weird circumstances. Ny had smoothed it over, yes, but it didn't mean the smoothing would go smoothly. Life and death were messy.

"Our insurance stuff. Deb's family. God, her funeral," I said, each phrase making more and more breath leave my body.

Merry reached out. "I'll take care of it all, Randy. I know what's what. I already have access to all your employee and financial info. I can handle it."

I squeezed her hand in thanks, unable to get it out around the grief clogging my throat. I felt Ny's hand on my shoulder. He'd moved closer to me without me even noticing. "Time also moves differently in the Dreamlands. What may take us days in the Dreamlands could have us returning within hours." I felt comforted for a beat, before Harley spoke.

"Meaning Mia's been gone far longer than two hours according to her perception?" Harley asked. Merry and I both gasped.

"Sadly, yes. Another reason Randy and I must travel quickly."

"I'm coming too." Gareth rose from his seat to stand straight with his feet planted shoulder width and his arms crossed, the usual Gareth-is-not-taking-no-for-an-answer stance.

"I don't even know if it's possible," I said, looking from him to Ny, who was already studying Gareth closely.

"Of all gathered here beyond the two of us," Ny said, "Gareth has the best chance of also crossing over. He's connected with our magic before on several occasions, managed to store it and use it when necessary. He is also a dream walker, meaning he's experienced transitions between planes of awareness. We can try. Although, bringing Gareth along will cause our entry to occur in a space more liminal, farther away from where we need to be for answers and proper transport within the Dreamlands."

Gareth took Ny's words in, then softened. "If it makes things more difficult, slower in some way, it might be best I stay behind."

"I think you could be of use, but I'll leave the final decision to Randy," Ny said.

Everyone looked at me, and I thought about it, really thought about it for a long, quiet minute. We needed to get to Mia ASAP, but who knew what was going on, what we would have to face, and how hard it might be? Mia needed us now, but she needed us prepared. Seemed to me, the more people, the better chance we had in whatever fight we faced. A part of me also wanted Gareth's calm along with me in all this craziness.

"I say he comes if he can."

"We need to talk about Nate." Harley's words were a stab to the gut because they so closely echoed Deb's from just hours before. When she had been alive.

"I can't. Not now," I muttered. "I agree he needs a chat, but I can't do it."

"I can," Merry said. "I know more now; I can talk with him about some basics of magic, or, at least, the basic fact magic is a thing and he seems to have some. He knows me better, so it might come better from me, anyway."

"I'll talk with him... but not until after." I couldn't do it then. No time and no patience.

All settled for the time, I rose without words, hugged my sister when she met me, and stumbled to my bed to lie in the dark. I was sleepless but silent for a time, content to let others take the reins before I had to step up again.

THE PLAN, A TANGIBLE goal I could focus on as a means to get Mia back, helped me breathe through the pain slicing up my insides. It helped dull the ache and sadness enough for me to function. Mainly because Mia needed me to function in order to carry out said plan and get her back to this plane, and I'd move heaven, earth, and all the Dreamlands to get my sister back. I'd walk into the lion's den, so to speak, without fear. It also helped my lion and my mage would prowl beside me, and I'd experienced the magic we created together. With it, finding and saving her didn't seem like too big of a task.

Ny had said he needed to test locations for entry. I knew he didn't want to return to the Dreamlands just yet, for a variety of reasons, but he was doing it for Mia. For me. My heart clenched over his unquestioning willingness and loyalty. He was an Outer God, but he was my Outer God. He'd proven it in small and big ways on the daily, and it was something I couldn't deny. At this point, I didn't want to deny it. I wanted to embrace it.

Same with Gareth. He'd been there from the beginning, his calm and knowledge and certainty in the face of all this swirling madness an anchor for me in this brave new world. Now he was willingly venturing out to lands where few humans went, from where even fewer humans returned according to Ny and Harley, without hesitation. Again, for Mia and for me.

These were the thoughts rattling around my skull as Harley, Gareth, and I poured over the books Harley had in her library on the Necronomicon and the Dreamlands. It brought tears to my eyes again, but they were good tears. I dropped the book I'd been holding onto the small wooden table the three of us were gathered around. The book landed with a thud, causing the piles of old tomes to jostle and shake and bringing both Harley's and Gareth's eyes to me.

"Gareth," I whispered, hoarse from my crying, past and present, and my emotions.

Harley held her eyes on me a moment but didn't waste time folding up from her chair with her lithe grace and wandering over to her wall of books. Maybe she needed to look for something new, but I figured it was to give me and Gareth some semblance of privacy.

Gareth's eyes shone at me, and I basked in their hazel light so like sunlight filtered through a lush forest scene. "Randy. It'll be okay."

"Possibly." A bit firmer, I said, "I have to believe it will be." I reached out to clasp his big, tattooed hands in mine. I stared down at our fingers intertwined, and I imagined our spirits or souls or whatever they could be called were now mingled all together in some way I didn't want to voice just yet, even if I felt it in my gut. I stayed staring there, not looking up at him. "You don't have to do this, you know. Ny and I can handle it. It'd be much safer if you stayed behind and helped here."

My hand rose, my arm pulled taut. Gareth was standing tall over me, pulling me up and into his body to hug me tightly. He whispered in my ears, "I helped Mia with the damned book." I jerked, knowing from the scrape and scratch of his voice he meant this as some sort of sordid confession. "No, Randy. Listen. I helped Mia with the book, assured you she would be safe, and

I was wrong. So very wrong. I can't... I can't take that back, my action, but I can help get Mia back. I can walk by you and Ny as you use whatever massive power you have to save her. Maybe even use some of my own tricks to help along the way. I'd do it for you regardless, but more importantly, I owe it to Mia."

I managed to tilt my head so I could look into his bearded face, so fierce and determined and sad. "I know a lot of us feel like the blame game would land firmly in our square right about now. You can't take it out on yourself, Gareth."

"Agree to disagree," he grumbled.

I shook my head and left it alone. I had my own mountain of guilt I wasn't about to let go of any time soon, so who was I to try to force him to let go of his own? Maybe he needed the fight, the action, to help alleviate it. We'd talk more about it again, I knew. There was no point doing it then because we had bigger issues. Like finding all we could in Harley's books to help us in this quest we were about to go on. And it was a quest. Definitely a quest for my sister. Possibly a quest to help get Ny's powers back and find out more about me and my own magics. Who knew what would happen? All I knew was whatever we'd face, good or bad, I'd do it with a mage, a prince, and my shadows at my side.

Eleven

DD SWOOPED AND SWIRLED around my head, a clear outward expression of my nervousness. DD felt it, echoed it, made me believe I wasn't simply being a coward. Going into the Dreamlands was a big fucking deal for sure, even with its Prince leading the way.

My sweaty palms might also give me away. Gareth was kind enough not to comment on it as Harley drove us and Merry to Union Cemetery, the same sprawling burial place where Ny and I had had our first official lesson in shades and shadows. It might've squeezed my heart with nostalgia if my empty stomach wasn't threatening to dry-heave at any moment.

We rolled slowly through the grounds, ending at a spot next to a small group of oaks, maples, and elms crowded around a giant weeping willow swaying in the slight August breeze. Ny stood, tall and stiff-backed, outside the hem of the swaying green curtain of branches and leaves. He waited patiently as Harley threw her sleek black sedan in park.

I didn't make to leave because I wanted to say something. Anything. My voice wouldn't come. Merry's voice didn't come at first either. She simply turned in her seat and reached a hand back, offering a clasp of care and love as I swallowed back tears yet again.

Harley didn't turn toward Gareth and me in the back, but she snagged our gazes in the rearview as she said, "No foolishness. You get in and you all get out. Hear me?"

I nodded. Gareth rumbled his assurances beside me. I was too focused on Merry to pay attention to what he said.

"You bring her home. You both come home." My sister sent abnormally stern glares at me and Gareth.

"Promise, Merry Berry." I squeezed her hand hard, and I couldn't say if it was more to comfort her or me.

She gave a hard, determined nod, then turned back to hide her tears falling. I still knew they fell by the slump of her shoulders and the shake of her head.

Gareth squeezed my other hand and said, "Ready?"

I wasn't. Likely wouldn't ever be ready to step into the Dreamlands with all I'd heard and imagined about the place. Mia hadn't been ready either, and she'd been dragged there kicking and screaming right in front of me, so I steeled myself and opened the car door. My foot had barely touched pavement when I was stopped by Harley's call.

"Randy. Remember what we talked about," she said, finally turning my way so I saw the serious dip of her face. We'd talked about a lot, Harley and I, but I knew she referenced the quick, hushed words she'd given me when we were alone for a moment in her hallway.

She'd quietly pulled me aside, away from Gareth and Merry after we'd come up empty in her library and Ny had slipped out to prepare. "You don't know what you'll find there, or how long you'll be there. Stick with Ny. Trust your gut and what the magic inside of you says. It won't lead you wrong. And please, for the love of anything possibly holy, answer your sister if she calls down your connection."

I'd barked a laugh at the last part, knowing Harley had told Merry we had no way of knowing if our bond worked in the Dreamlands but she was free to try. Now, minutes away from leaving Columbus and the entirety of the human plane of existence, I hoped like hell it did work, that I could have her voice in my head if or when I needed it.

I gave her no words. Instead, I swiftly exited and walked around the other side of the car to join Gareth waiting on the edge where grass met black road. I looked back to give Merry what I hoped was a jaunty, reassuring wave. It likely didn't work because I didn't feel jaunty or reassured myself, so I quickly made my way deeper into the grass as I tried not to think about the sound of Harley's car crunching rocks as it drove away.

Gareth was a silent, calming warmth behind me as we strode up to Ny. I hadn't even thought about what I needed to wear before donning a basic tee and some jeans and my big black combat boots. Gareth was dressed pretty much the same, though it was his usual attire. Ny looked like Ny, skinny dark jeans and white tee and black jacket.

"Are you both ready?" he asked, eyeing us humans up and down. He shrugged out of the jacket and draped it over me, either for warmth or whatever protection his scent might offer.

"As ready as we can be for interdimensional travel, I guess," I said, pushing my arms through the body-warmed leather and pulling my long, dark hair from under the collar and shaking it out down my back.

Gareth said nothing.

Ny didn't waste time. He gestured toward the weeping willow and gave us his instructions. "This is the closest gateway I found. The edge of the tree in the cemetery gives us an entry point. Zoog gather here, so it should be a solid point for any dream walker to enter. However…" He pulled the old pocket watch out of his leather jacket and handed it to Gareth. "Draw from this now, but do not siphon all the magic at once. You may need more before our journey is complete. Take enough so you can use our shadow power to help you slip with us into the in-between."

"The plan is we jump from here, to this in-between spot, then into the Dreamlands?" I asked.

"Yes. It will keep us together and not drain as much power. We follow the willow line, then the zoog, and both will lead us true."

"What are zoog?" I asked, right as a tiny brown crea-ture darted out in front of us. I stiffened, thinking of rat-man John and what other horrors I may encounter.

Ny stepped back to lay a steadying hand on my shoulder. He made a clicking sound, a call in an alien language, and the darting brown body zipped toward us. It stopped at our feet and looked up with black, beady eyes. The rodent-like body was smooth and hair-less, almost shining in glints of bronze and copper. Beautiful in its oddity and coloring. It clicked up at Ny, who answered in their language. He had a whole-ass conversation with the small animal body occasionally gesturing with its head here and there. Finally, it scur-ried to the edge of the leafy willow curtain and stopped to throw what very much appeared to be an impatient look over its slick shoulder.

"Come," Ny said, stepping between Gareth and me to take our hands in his. "We must hurry and we must step through together."

"What's our intention?" Gareth asked, his voice low and slightly unsure, something I'd never heard coming from him. It made both me and DD rattle with con-cern.

Ny paused, gathering his thoughts before he spoke. "Complex. For me, I will think of the Dreamlands, as they are my home. My intention to return, which always works well for me. You and Randy should con-centrate on finding two very different things, either of which should guide you true: Mia and the part of the Dreamlands both of you have seen, the Writhing."

"The Writhing?" I asked, even though I was pretty sure I knew what he meant.

"The tentacled shadows you've encountered in real life and in dreams. Those are a physical part of the Dreamlands you've experienced; therefore, they can serve as a point of intention to help you bridge the gap between here and the in-between."

"Okey doke," I said. It was again meant to be playful, but I was too serious, too nervous to make it sound anything but flat and hesitant.

We paused directly in front of the gently swaying line of willow branches and leaves in full summer green. I could see shadowy grass and trunks beyond but barely. Instead of focusing on what was there, I turned my intention as Ny had instructed. I thought of Mia—sassy, infuriating, lovely, Mia—and my burning desire to get to her. I wrapped the thought in shadows, in my power, and in wisps of imagined, darker tentacles I'd used in real life and in dreams.

Ny took one step, then another, and we matched him on either side. I felt a pull from DD, a weight added to it at my side, and knew it tried its best to also help us along. Tiny steps forward, until the leaves brushed our feet, then our faces. I felt them caress, almost hold, and it was like the branches breathed out in release as we moved through the curtain to find a whole new world at our feet.

I couldn't say more about the magic making it possible for me to step between worlds as easily as I stepped from the café to the kitchen in Warm Regards. It seemed like it should have been a bigger thing—a production with sparks and stars and some pain—given what I had felt when I'd first shadow walked. Apparently unmaking wasn't a part of this for me, thankfully. I felt the weight of DD tethered to me like a helium balloon pulling a string tight. I sensed my inner magic grow and stretch, shadows churning up from my gut. My skin marked the change in air, a dip in temperature and humidity and something else unknown and unnamable adding to the caress of it across my cheeks, almost the same as the weight of salt in the air at the ocean but without the grit and scratch. My skin touched the new world, marked it as different, even before my nose and eyes registered more. That was all I registered and understood. Magic, even my magic, was still too new and unused to be able to fully untangle all it did to get me from one realm into the other.

What I could sense better than most, taste, helped because I could roll the thick atmosphere around on my tongue. My palate was trained to break apart small bits and pieces and find the truth, figure out what was what in any given dessert or pastry. It did the same in the new plane, taking in the taste of the air and parceling out what was what. I tasted magic, my own dark undertones and Ny's electric spiciness. Even a tinge of Gareth's earthy notes. Other magic hung in the air, magic I didn't know and couldn't describe other than to say the taste reminded me of smothered fires, wet woods, and, oddly enough, pomegranate.

I didn't know what any of it actually meant, and I wasn't about to ask more detailed questions in the moment because I realized Gareth was grunting in pain on the other side of Ny.

"Don't let go," Ny said in a smooth command, not looking at me. "Keep my hand tight."

I wasn't sure if he meant me or Gareth, but I wasn't about to test it out by not doing as he told. I did ask, possibly a bit shrill and not at all cool, "What's happening?" as I craned my body around Ny's to try to catch a glimpse of Gareth.

I saw him on his knees, clinging to Ny with one hand, his back arched and his other hand clamped over his mouth to stifle his groans.

"Center yourself. Focus on intention. Breathe through the pain. It will fade, I promise you."

"Did you know this would happen?" I demanded.

Not sparing a look at me, Ny answered, "Know for certain? No. Suspect it as a possibility? Yes."

"You didn't think to tell us?" I shrieked, worry for Gareth snaking up my stomach, threatening to strangle me.

"Calm yourself..."

"You may have had sexy times with lots of human women, Prince," I spat back, "but you don't know shit about them if you think 'calm down' is the right thing to say to any woman with a valid complaint about something you did. Or failed to do, in this case."

By this time, Gareth was able to speak through loud breaths between clenched teeth. "I'm okay, Randy. Just need a minute."

Ny cocked his head at me, his eyes darker here, his power testing the bounds of his human form, pleading to be let out in this familiar place. An odd echo sounded in his voice too. It made the hair on my body stand on end.

"Apologies, Randy. I see your points. However, can we discuss your complaint at another time?"

I nodded, staring at Ny's back as he twisted again to comfort Gareth, guide him through the pain. Eventually he got him there, maybe through magic or maybe through his voice. After a long ten minutes, Gareth staggered up to his feet. He swayed slightly, but he stood. A good sign.

"We have to keep up the hand holding?" I asked at this point.

"Best to do so until we reach the Dreamlands beyond this forest."

His words, and Gareth's assurances that most of his pain was gone, made me finally take in my surroundings. We definitely weren't in the cemetery anymore. We were in a forest, like Ny had said—an ancient forest with trees I didn't recognize, dotted with iridescent moss. The occasional Dayglo mushroom, like something out of a bad acid trip, popped out of the black soil here and there. There was no discernible path, only acres and acres of trees surrounding the odd circular clearing where we stood.

"It's like a landing pad in an alien forest."

"Not far off, sweetling," Ny affirmed before tugging my arm for attention. He must have tugged us both because I noticed Gareth turn to face Ny at the same time.

"This is the in-between plane situation as a gateway for the Dreamlands and the human realm. It is the home of the zoog, who are able to flit between so they can guard entry if necessary. Humans aren't barred, per se, but as you found, it often takes a good deal of power, at a particular bodily cost, for them to enter. I'd hoped our gathered power would have been enough to offset it, but it still took a toll. I am sorry my assumption was incorrect, Gareth."

Gareth shook out his arms as if shaking away the pain. His sigils flared in the odd gray gloom of the place as he spoke. "It's done. Will the transition to the Dreamlands be the same? If so, I may need to siphon more power before I make the journey."

"No. The first phase is the largest hurdle. Besides, the Dreamlands wants me back and will help ease our way at this point."

"So we can get going?" I wasn't too worried about logistics as long as it got us where we needed to go.

Ny pulled us forward and stepped in answer, and Gareth and I followed in his wake, trying to take the same steps as him or as close as our position as an oddly joined trio allowed. I stayed on track for the most part, not allowing my eyes to wander. Zoog were there, scurrying around and giving clicks to Ny on occasion, communicating things I couldn't guess.

I looked around a bit, enough to notice darker and larger eyes looking back in the gray dark between trees, in trees, and on trees. Eyes in sets of two, four, six. Once, so many were clustered together peering my way, I couldn't count them before I turned my head and shuddered at the absurdity and horror of it. Ny held firm, so I felt safe, but only just.

It didn't help when Ny muttered, "Pay them no mind. Much more frightening creatures inhabit the dark up ahead." Not at all comforting, but I guess good to know. Vigilance and all that.

Not going to lie, I stumbled a few times over roots and bumps. Even almost stepped on a zoog before it let out a squeak I could clearly interpret as "watch yourself." Still, I never let go of Ny's hand. Held a death grip on the thing.

After what felt like miles, I saw a break in the trees ahead. A clearing of sorts loomed, and once we were close enough, I saw what it was: a circle of stone mono-liths. It was like Stonehenge, except there weren't tops to the stone grouping. Or, at least, not tops I could see. In fact, the stones reached so high up in the sky I couldn't see the tops anyway.

Ny came to a halt on one side, turning his head in the scenting, jerky-yet-still-fluid feline manner he had when he scented the air. "Yes," he said. "Here."

Gareth and I didn't question him. We waited for more info or instructions. For my part, I didn't say much because it was all too new, too real, and too raw for me. All I could do was step when asked, perform the task in front of me, and hope it led me to my sister.

Ny eventually tightened his grip on my hand and said, with the odd echo still in his voice, "We walk into the Dreamlands here."

I pulled in a deep breath of air, filling my lungs with its odd caress and weight, and Ny tugged us, half a step behind him, into his realm.

Twelve

Of course my first step into the Dreamlands would be a stumble. To be fair, one second we were breathing thick air in a gray gloom of a forest, wading through it in a way I wasn't thinking too much about, and the next it was a clear, bright day on the outskirts of a field that looked like it could've been in the middle of rural Ohio, farmers and all. The handful of people a dozen yards or so in the distance, who looked positively human, only glanced in our direction before returning to their work. At least they didn't stop to gawk at my near face-plant.

Ny's sure grip kept me upright. He'd moved in his lightning-quick way, pulling our still-connected arms taut so I sprang back before I ate a face full of dirt. "Thanks," I muttered halfheartedly as I squinted in the light, searching the farmland in front of us.

There were no magic shadows except for DD radiating solid strength at my side. Regular noonday shadows peeked out here and there, like on any sunny day in the human realm, but I'd expected a much darker place. The fields rippled in a gentle breeze, the crops which at first glance looked like soybeans in size and color throwing off a faint shimmer as they moved in the light. Enough to mark them as something outside the human realm. Enough to make me believe we really were in the Dreamlands and not back in Ohio somewhere.

"What…" I couldn't finish. There were too many questions to pinpoint. This field was definitely not anything like I had imagined when I'd thought about the Dreamlands, the place where my dark Ny ruled.

"There are people," Gareth whispered, and I moved to see an astonished look on his face. I was sure mine looked the same.

Almost flippantly—offhandedly, as he was busy taking in our surroundings and likely concocting some plan in his head—Ny said, "Of course. Those humans who survive the crossing don't all perish immediately. There are people, farmers, towns, cities. There are humans and other creatures very like humans who inhabit my realm. It is a realm like so many others, full of life, magic, and danger in equal measure."

Feeling a little shitty about my assumptions about the Dreamlands, I stopped gawking at the farmers and took a look at where we stood. We'd stepped through in an in-between place, as Ny liked to call it, to a little strip where field met grass which then met a few trees.

He pulled us gawking humans into the shade of a tree before letting go of our hands. His immediately went to my face, cupping it. "Are you well?"

"Peachy." I took a moment to reach out to DD, who hovered close to my side, to make sure it was okay. DD seemed more than okay. Calmed and maybe even happy. Guessed the Dreamlands were good for it, which gave me one less thing to worry about. I called it closer, so it rested at my shoulder. No sense borrowing trouble and letting DD get too far away. It never had before, unless I sent it out, but we were in a new place and space and maybe even time and there was no telling what could happen.

Ny moved to Gareth, not exactly touching him fully but skimming his hand across his torso, feeling him out with something other than touch. "Are you well, friend? Feeling better?"

Gareth's shoulders bunched and twisted. He stretched his neck, flexed his arms and fingers, stomped his feet in quick successions, and blinked, and a few of his sigils glowed with Ny's dark light. He tested his body and magic stores before he answered. "Yes. I seem to be fine."

"Good. Good," Ny said, before starting off across the fields, out into a distance I couldn't see. I didn't know if he was actually seeing something or thinking. Probably both, given the pinched look on his face. It smoothed when he turned toward us.

"We have little time and a great deal of ground to cover. There are a few things you must know before we proceed."

If it was anything like the pain Gareth had buckled under when we'd reached the place of the zoog, then I was all ears, especially since Ny's usually smooth voice still held an off-kilter internal echo. Truth be told, it made the magic thrum in me pulse to its underlying bass beat.

Ny continued. "I have additional power here but am still well below my normal range without the Book of Knowing and the power it holds. Most will not notice. I've ruled here long enough for no one to question or confront me outright without proof. However, the person who commanded Wilbur is here. Whoever they are, they will know my weaknesses. We must be vigilant and swift. Add to this neither of you are from the Dreamlands, are unfamiliar with this place and its magics, and there could be much danger ahead. I need you to follow my lead here, and do so without hesitation." By the end of his warning, his voice had leveled out as he got reacquainted to the space and power in the Dreamlands. It melded into something like his voice in the Dreamlands with an added hint of rumble, a magic timbre giving his already strong voice more heft.

Gareth and I didn't say anything. I was mesmerized by his changing voice. Maybe Gareth was too. We eventually both nodded, but Ny's eyes stayed on mine. "Sweetling, this means you may need to rein in your comebacks."

Gareth eyed me as well, and my fascination with Ny's voice shifting was wiped away by my annoyance at what he'd implied.

I threw my hands in the air. "What? You think I'm stupid? This place may look very Ohio, but believe you me, I know it definitely is not. We need to get to Mia ASAP. You're the best way we can do that and get her back from whatever evil clutches she's fallen into, so yeah. I'll zip it." I thought for a moment and corrected myself. "I'll zip it as much as I possibly can."

Gareth's answering cough sounded an awful lot like a stifled laugh. Ny wasn't even trying to hide his shit-eating grin. I huffed and rolled my hand. "Please, oh great Prince. Continue."

He gave a mocking bow at the use of his title, his usual flippancy and joking manner soothing me in this new place where his magic felt even stronger, more charged, than in the human realm. Ny used a hand at each of our backs to turn us toward the open field. With a flick of his head, he directed our gaze up, over a smattering of more distant trees and across the white expanse of sky. It was the first time I noticed the white sky, similar to our own but leeched of color. It grayed and darkened as we looked out toward something I couldn't really see in the distance.

"We must travel to Ulthar. There, the two of you will need to enter the city by yourselves in order to meet with a particular priest. He and I have a certain history and a formal relationship, which makes it necessary for you to question him alone. However, I know he will help you despite our past. He is our safest and quickest means for discovering where Mia may be hidden in this realm."

My stomach dipped. "It's so far away." I couldn't even see the Ulthar place he talked about. It'd take days, at least, to get there.

"Distance in my realm is relative."

"Like time?" I asked. Always back to the physics with him.

"Yes, sweetling. Like time, space and distance are a matter of means and ability here." He dipped a hand and coaxed a shadow from the tree line, making it larger and darker with every passing second.

Worried about Gareth, I asked, "Are we shadow walking?"

He shook his head no. "Gareth can hold our power, but he does not have all of our abilities. Shadow walking is beyond him. We will be riding the shadow."

"Like a magic carpet?" I asked, thinking about Aladdin.

Ny smiled at me, offered his hand, and asked, "Do you trust me?"

I barked out a laugh. Gareth joined in. The Prince of the Dreamlands looked a little like Aladdin, though hotter, but it was absurd to think the two were anything alike. Just as absurd as imagining Crawling Chaos quoting a Disney movie at you.

The shadow formed a floating circle, obviously made to fit the three of us. "Come," Ny said, stepping onto the shadow first. It didn't hover off the ground like a magic carpet, but it was a solid slip on the earth, something rippling with each of his steps but still solid beneath his feet.

I shrugged and stepped on, feeling the give of the shadow. It felt and looked like a taut trampoline, and I had a fleeting thought about trying to bounce on it before I squashed the idea real quick. Gareth followed me on, and the shadow adjusted accordingly. Then I felt it more deeply, in the pit of me, the piece of me Ny said was made of shadow. I knew it would answer to me if I called it, like DD answered. Like the tentacles answered. Ny cocked his head in question but I shook mine at him. He was piloting this thing, not me.

"If you would feel more comfortable, you can hold on to me," Ny offered as he turned his body away from me and Gareth.

Gareth didn't hesitate, landing a large hand on Ny's left shoulder and gripping it tight from behind. I followed too, though I wrapped my arm in Ny's right, moving tight into his side before lacing our fingers together.

"This okay?" I asked. Didn't want to keep his hand occupied if he needed it to move us along.

"Always," he said with his cattish smile, the one a touch too sharp and shiny, before I felt us move, and we were traveling in the shadows across a strangely familiar land.

THE MAGIC SHADOW RIDE was an odd experience, but there were a whole bunch of odd experiences in Ny's realm. The shadow propelled us forward, but not like the steady, easy glide of a car or plane. We hopped from shadow to shadow, so quick it caused our bodies to bang and lurch, fighting against the movement until we got the hang of it. I'd been to NYC a few times, and this felt an awful lot like riding the subway when it was a new experience: jerky motion mixed with frequent stops and large bursts of speed that were only really felt when looking out the windows. Not having any windows on the shadow ride was not an improvement on the experience.

The realm passed by, too quickly to take real notice of our surroundings beyond momentary stops. There were blurs of color, then a field. Another blur of light and color, then we were under a redwood tree taller than any I'd seen in pictures; I'd never actually seen one in real life, so I couldn't rightly compare. More blurs then a stop at the edge of some lake, the water a silvery color rippling and pulsing with its own beat. I wasn't one to get motion sick, up until this. It was a bit much. Eventually I simply closed my eyes and let my body sway with the movement, using my lock on Ny's arm as an anchor.

What felt like hours later, we stopped and didn't bolt again. Ny squeezed my hand in his, and I peeked through one cracked eye.

"We're here."

I noticed the firmness beneath the shadow at my feet, the stillness of the darkness rippling with my slight movements. We were stationary and, from Ny's words, at our destination. I uncurled myself from Ny's side and looked for Gareth to make sure he was okay. He met my gaze with a soft smile and nod. He'd obviously been looking for assurance from me too, so I gave a wink before turning in a circle to peek at our surroundings.

It was a little disappointing at first. We stood on a non-descript gravel road made of black, oily rock, situated in the middle of an open expanse of field—not a farmer-type field but barrenness. Nothingness as far as the eye could see. I made a one-eighty and saw the rising city behind me, teeming with light and sound and movement all around. I wasn't one to judge distance well, but we were close to it. Maybe a mile away.

It was still light out, which was good. However, the light white was dipping into soft gray, with true blackness creeping around the edges. Night was coming in quick.

"We'll go directly to the gate in a moment," Ny said, "but we need to stop and discuss a few important issues first."

I wanted to ask why but also didn't want to give up on my promise to follow his lead just yet. Ny saw the conflict in my eyes and gave me the answer without the question anyway.

"You're not simply seeing a priest. He is the Oracle of Ulthar. As such, he holds great power in the city. Technically, not more power than I hold, but a great deal of power nonetheless. We've had issues in the past. It is best we bypass such issues by taking me out of the equation. I get closer to the city, stay longer than necessary to leave you and Gareth at its gates, the Oracle will know and will comment. May even take offense I didn't petition for help in a formal manner—something we definitely do not have time for, given our current need."

"Okay. You drop us off and wait for us somewhere else."

"Yes. Here." He paused a moment, then continued. "Ulthar is a city, and like all cities, it holds certain dangers if you are unfamiliar with its quirks. Same with all of the Dreamlands. I know the two of you can hold your own in the human realm; however, there are things in this world you cannot fathom. I will send protectors to walk with you while you venture into Ulthar. These protectors are fierce warriors revered throughout most of the Dreamlands. Few would dare bother you in their presence."

"How will we know who they are?" Gareth asked, always ready with the smart questions.

"They will bear my name and title."

"Great. We have warriors coming to help and we need to talk to an oracle. All good. What, exactly, do we need to talk to the Oracle about? I mean, I know we're talking about Mia, but is there a particular way we should approach this dude with our questions?"

Ny shook his head. "The Oracle will know who you are and what you want. He'll know why you're there and that you travel with me. All I do now is to try to mitigate these factors, make it so he may look on you more favorably. He's also not an evil being. Ask him openly and honestly whatever you wish to know; do not hold back details about Mia and your desire to find her because of your love for her."

"Anything else?" I asked, trying to make sure we covered all our bases.

"Remember to say nothing of me unless asked. Also, under no circumstances should you let the Oracle know about my missing power."

"Got it. Open and honest about Mia. Hush hush about you." I stepped between my guys and hugged each to one side. "Let's get this thing moving again. We have an oracle to question. Maybe some spoons to bend."

Gareth chuckled at the reference, and I marveled at the fact Ny made a Disney joke but not one about *The Matrix*. Only for a second though, because soon we were flitting over shadows to the gates of Ulthar and any answers Gareth and I could find there.

Thirteen

I'D ONLY BEEN TO Europe once, and it had been to spend two weeks in Paris on a patisserie tour with some of my pastry chef friends right after we graduated. There'd been lots of wine, lots of sweets, and we'd skipped the sightseeing beyond the mandatory trips to the Eiffel Tower and the Louvre. I thought about my lack of travel experience outside of the US when Ny dropped us off at the gates of Ulthar. They were literal gates—large wood and metal doors towering overhead at least twenty feet and connected to a thick wall of slick, glittering stone. It made me think of medieval European castles from movies, which I'd never seen in real life.

However, the doors were open, and all manner of people wandered in and out as the white skies slowly faded into what I assumed was the dark or the Dreamland version of dusk, then night. The chatter was the normal hum of any group going about their business, although the few times I heard an English word, it was punctuated by languages I didn't recognize at all.

"Let's go," Gareth said after he scoped out the entrance.

I grabbed his hand and let him lead, mostly because he knew more about magic than I did and I could feel magic humming in the air here, something less hidden and more readily used. Or potentially more readily used. I didn't know the etiquette of blasting strangers with magic in this realm, and I wasn't about to test it. Best to keep my head down and hold tight to Gareth as he wove his way through the dispersing gate crowd, up wide cobblestone streets lined with tall stone structures, some with shops and markets bustling, and some which could've been houses or apartments of sorts. It wasn't all too different from the older parts of Columbus actually. Well, except for the variety of non-humans about and the magic taste in the thick air. The other difference was the looming center we moved toward—a large, glittering stone structure Ny told us housed the Oracle.

I'd like to say everything was out of the ordinary, but it wasn't. Ulthar was like cities all over the human realm. There were tall buildings, walkways, and roads. People moved quickly to wherever they were going, not really paying much attention to others. There were vehicles, though they weren't cars. More like small, sparking flatbeds moving in more directions than forward and reverse. It was a place with people, and if it wasn't for the differences in tech and language, and the feel of magic across my skin, I could've said it was any city in the world.

Just like with any city in the world, it wasn't great when not knowing the way around. Soon enough, we came to a smaller street, possibly an alley. The shadows there were dark and long, and the sounds of things slithering across the stones ahead did not make me enthusiastic about venturing farther down it.

Gareth stopped when I tugged his hand. He looked back at me and asked, "Are you okay?"

"This may not be the best way to go."

He swung his head as if just then taking in his surroundings, a luxury he may have had because he held power and magic and was a white dude who lived a Midwestern city. He wasn't nearly as safe here, and he should've walked more cautiously.

He pointed up, where the building constructed from the same stone as the wall around the city rose high above us, straight ahead. "I get your point, Randy, but we're both unsure here. It might be better if we take the most direct route."

"You don't know it's a direct route, Gareth. You assume. There could be a dead end in twenty feet and you can't see it through all the darkness in this oddly deserted, slightly menacing-looking alleyway thing."

He cocked his head. "You think we should stick to major roads, even if it takes us longer to get there, leaving us in this unknown city for longer?"

"Yes." My assertion was punctuated with great dramatic timing by the clatter of metal on stone up ahead, making me and DD jump to high alert immediately. Gareth moved in front of me, as if to protect me. I appreciated it, but if something magic was coming our way, me and DD might be better help, so I moved us beside the now gently glowing mage.

DD was still, waiting. Not in a tense way, like me. It was far more Zen. More as if it knew what was coming and wasn't worried about it, which in turn made me less tense, but only a little less. Until a tiny black kitten scampered out of the inky darkness of the alley, letting out a screeching meow as it barreled toward us.

I should've probably been more cautious, but it was a kitten. All tiny body and big belly and downy black fur with its small tail standing straight into the air. If it was an attack, I was a goner. "Oh! It's a tiny baby!" I said before I knelt to scoop it into my hands. The little black nose, cold and slick, nudged my chin before it rubbed its head along my jawline and turned on its little purr engine. I felt a tiny cord around its neck, a collar of sorts, as I gave it good scritches and cooed to it. DD bounced down to investigate, and the little thing tried to paw it. DD didn't seem to mind, wiggling as if also totally taken by the cuteness of the thing.

"Randy," Gareth said. It wasn't a chastisement or an attempt to get his own pets in with the cute creature. It was a cautious call to pay attention to something other than the tiny purring furnace snuggling in my arms.

I looked up, and he was staring ahead, his body tight and sigils flaring.

When I saw where he focused, I understood. About two dozen cats of all shapes and sizes were gathered in front of us. Some kittens like the little one in my arms, some spry teenage cats, some mature. Some were larger than any house cat I'd seen in the human realm. Those looked more like bobcats except they had long, sleek tails they swished in the air behind them. None made a sound; they only stood or sat, peering up at us with their assessing, slightly condescending feline gazes, which, when I got over the shock, definitely reminded me of something. Or more like someone.

I held the kitten up to my face and asked it, "Who sent you?" right before it playfully booped my nose with its tiny paw. I brought its collar close to my face to read the small medallion suspended there. It was a bronze-like disk with substantial weight and had the words "Prince Nyarlathotep" stamped alongside symbols I couldn't decipher.

I let out a laugh. "Seems these are our protectors," I said to Gareth, holding the kitten and its collar up so he could also read the inscription dangling from the thing.

"Fitting, I suppose," Gareth grumbled, eyeing the cats in front of us warily.

"Sure is. Also, absurdly cute." I gave the kitten a small kiss on the head, which made it rear back in pure catlike affront at my audacity. A laugh bubbled out and

I talked to it. "Fine, young warrior. I sure am honored to have a protector as cute as you." I set it down and it trotted back to the group of cats assembled before us as if joining their ranks.

"Prince Nyarlathotep sent you?" Gareth asked. I wondered for a second if they spoke English until one of the bobcat-sized ones, a big orange-striped cat with a small chunk taken from one ear, stepped forward, sat, and gave a small dip of its head and a slow blink at us.

"Oh, the slow blink. A good sign," I told Gareth.

"What?"

"Slow blinking in cats means they trust you."

"O-kay," he said slowly, before blowing out a breath and easing some of the tension in his body. "Okay. Our protectors are a bunch of cats."

"I'm fine with it. Cats don't play."

Gareth nodded, surveyed the group in front of us, then asked, "What is the quickest, safest way to the Oracle?"

The big orange boy stood and trotted toward and around us, a small portion of the others jumping to follow him closely. Others waited and watched, I assumed to take a protective position behind us. "Seems I was right," I said, more than a little smug.

Gareth didn't reply. He took my hand in his and we walked in the circle of cats down the street. I noticed people steered clear, but I was unsure if it was the oddity of seeing so many cats with two randos or something else. Didn't much matter. Right then, I was focused on following the straight tails of those cats to the all-knowing Oracle for some different answers.

THE LARGE BUILDING WE entered looked more like a government building than some mystical stronghold where an oracle would dole out wisdom. It had a few widows toward the top of its massive tower, but for the most part, it was uninterrupted slabs of the same glittery, slightly wet looking stone from the Ulthar gates rising at least thirty stories. One small door at the bottom stood open. No gate or even door was there to close it up if needed, at least not one I could see as we followed the cats into what appeared to be a stone waiting room. It was a brightly lit space lined with stone benches, where all manner of people and creatures sat trying not to stare awkwardly at each other as they waited their turn. I half expected to see one of those round red ticket dispensers below a digital sign reading "Now serving #87" somewhere in the room, but nope. People waited without numbers for their turn at a talk with the Oracle.

While I'd scanned the room, the orange tabby leader of the cats had gone to meow at a person standing at a set of stairs. The person nodded as if they fluently spoke cat and beckoned Gareth and me over with a curled finger.

"You may enter," the person said, waving us up the stairs. We didn't even have to take a seat. The cats got us good service in Ulthar. Sadly, they left Gareth and me to do this bit on our own.

We marched up the stone staircase visible from the waiting area until it turned into an arch along the stone wall. A hallway and more stairs followed.

"Do we have to trudge all the way to the top? Because I don't know if my knees or glutes can take it," I grumbled at Gareth.

He chuckled but didn't reply. Both of us were in new territory, so he couldn't rightly answer me. Another turn past stone and another long hallway without doors led us to a large open space lined with fiery sconces. It was great ambiance for the white-haired, middle-aged guy sitting on a cushioned seat in the middle of the room.

"Ah. Miranda Carter and Gareth Davis. Nice to meet you in the flesh," he called, a bright and, I think, honest smile on his face.

"You know about us?" I blurted without thinking. DD bumped against me before going completely still, a soft and silent warning for me to remember what I was supposed to be doing.

"Of course I do, child. I wouldn't have much power if I could not even decern who would come to call on me for answers."

I bristled at the child thing but let it slide.

"Then you know why we've come," Gareth stated.

"I do. Both because I've foreseen part of your journey and I have heard word of the Necronomicon appearing once again in the Dreamlands."

"You've heard about my sister?" I asked, moving toward the man to make sure I heard every word he said about Mia.

He held up a hand to stop me, and I would have ignored it completely if Gareth hadn't grabbed my hand and held it fast. I blinked, about to argue, but thought better of it. I didn't know how this whole thing worked exactly, but I needed him to tell me more, and it was unlikely he'd spill if I offended him in some way. The size of the space, the drama of it, and the lushness of his silken robes and his cushioned chair all transmitted the idea he was someone who was used to others doing exactly as he said. I needed to tread lightly with this dude. I was super lucky I had DD and Gareth by my side to keep me on track and out of unintentional trouble.

"Yes. I have information regarding the book."

I gritted my teeth at him calling Mia a book again but held it in, held his gaze, and waited for him to keep going. "In dreams I have seen it, shrouded in deep clouds on top of a steep mountain."

"Can you tell us the name of this mountain?" Gareth asked before I could demand.

"I can." However, he stopped there, eyeing Gareth and me before he asked a question of his own. "Why did Prince Nyarlathotep not petition me himself?"

"He didn't want your past to cause us friction," Gareth answered.

"Plus, we're a little short on time to go through all the formal rigamarole." It was not the best thing to say, given the curl of his lip, but oh well. "We do need to find my sister as soon as possible."

"What will you sacrifice, Miranda Carter, to find the book?"

This dude was getting on my nerves already, with this Miranda and book business, and I wasn't in the mood for whatever games he was playing, so my voice was whip sharp with annoyance. "You mean my sister? My baby sister? The one I held right after she was born, her tiny life in my little-kid arms? The one who was ripped out of my arms by some evil fuckery, dragged into this world against her will? The one I love more than I love myself? Believe me, old man, when I say I'll do whatever's necessary to find her, to save her."

"What of him, or the Prince?"

"What about them?" I snapped back, confused.

He cocked his head in thought and didn't clarify anything, only stared at me. He blinked and, even from halfway across the space, I could see his eyes had morphed into all white spaces. They'd been non-descript before, but now it was like something straight out of a horror movie.

"You will give up much for your heart, and even then, I cannot guarantee you will acquire all you desire. However, it is good you learn the burden of sacrifice.

To love so fiercely is in itself a form of self-sacrifice, yet so much more will eventually be required of you, torchbearer."

That was condescending as hell, but I wasn't about to snark at Old White Eyes just then. Especially since he had some weird-ass name possibly connected to my lessons with Ny from months ago, which proved his bona fides as a seer of sorts.

He moved forward quickly, coming within steps of me before I could react. DD moved on its own to shield me, but the Oracle waved a dismissive hand at it, freezing it in midair. His sightless white eyes peered into me somehow, and I felt compelled to move forward myself, get closer, to hear every nuance of whatever it was he was about to say to me. Luckily, Gareth's death grip on my hand kept me close. "Be mindful of your becoming, Miranda Carter. You will have a choice, as all do. Choose wisely. Need and love drive you on now, as they should. It is the best way to evolve."

"Evolve?" It was an odd choice of words, and with someone like this, I figured word choice was important. I'd seen enough fantasy movies with prophesies in them to know as much.

"To grow. Shift. Evolve." He answered as if I were stupid, and I gave my own sneer. I knew the basic definition. I wanted more clarity. Guessed I wasn't getting it.

Cryptic messages about growth and evolution were all well and good but not why I was there. "Where is my sister?" I asked again.

In a flash, the Oracle's face was inches from my own, his white eyes unblinking and his voice hard when he said, "I tire of you. You are as arrogant and stubborn as your master, so it is time you run along to him."

Ny sure was arrogant and stubborn, but right then I figured this dude deserved it from him, so I didn't hold it against my guy. Although, I felt the need to clarify one point. "I have no master."

"Perhaps. Yet we all have masters, Miranda Carter. Be they someone else or parts of ourselves we cannot tame."

Weird and cryptic, but whatever. Again, I asked, "Where is my sister?" I bared my clenched teeth at the Oracle as I pushed out the words.

He tilted his head to look at Gareth and instead of answering said, "Watch where you step, Gareth Davis. Some falls have dire consequences."

I wondered if Gareth was about to trip or something, but his feet were firm and not close to anything trippable or any ledges I could see.

The Oracle gave a beleaguered sigh and looked at his feet as he said, "You will find the book on Kadath, a place few humans have ever tread, and even fewer have survived. Follow the Prince but do not trust the royals."

I nodded, ready to bolt without saying good-bye, when the Oracle grabbed my hand in his warm, bony grip. "How to become is as important as what you become, Miranda Carter." He pressed something in my hand before another blinding light flashed and he was seated once again, regular eyes, on his cushy seat. "You may run back to Prince Nyarlathotep now," he said, waving a super dismissive hand our way.

Okay then. I snorted and turned to leave. I didn't need to be told twice. In fact, I bolted as quickly as I could through the building and out the doors, Gareth and the crowd of protector cats on my tail.

Only when I was streets away, hidden in the dark, did I unclench my fist and looked at what the Oracle had given me. It was a silver key, as long as my palm was wide, with an ornate, curlicue head. Odd markings I couldn't read were etched across the surface. I turned it over and over and asked Gareth, "Know what this is?"

He held it, gasped at the feel, and I knew I wasn't mistaken. The thing radiated power—power like Ny radiated, which seemed not so great when it was connected to a random object.

Gareth pushed through the sensation and studied the markings closely. "They look like sigils, but I'm unfamiliar with their meaning or usage."

"Best ask Ny then," I said, taking the key to slide it in my tiny jeans pocket. Luckily it fit snuggly there, in the usually annoying and useless pockets they put into lady jeans.

"You think it's wise to keep it?" Gareth asked, eyeing my pants in a not-sexy way.

"It probably would be worse to randomly throw it out before talking to Ny about it."

"True. Speaking of..."

A meow, long and loud, sounded behind us, and we looked down to see the orange leader sitting at our feet, pure cat annoyance on its face. "Okay. Okay. Get us to Prince Nyarlathotep as quickly as possible."

It moved, gracefully and with purpose, into the lead, winding us through the city streets of Ulthar, toward our Outer God and, hopefully soon, my sister.

Fourteen

WE'D MADE IT ABOUT a hundred yards outside Ulthar's gates, surrounded all the while by our cat protectors, before Ny swooped in on his shadow. Night had fully fallen and the dark road and shadows bled together, so it seemed like he'd made a small step off of shadow and onto the road. I was definitely happy for it. We had a named location, so there were questions to answer and plans to make and a sister to rescue as soon as we could get to the Kadath place. Plus, it felt like something was hovering out of reach of my senses, like nasty creatures in the Dreamland darkness waiting for a chance to strike.

It didn't help that the dark here was so true and deep and unknowable. Night had fallen, and I'd never understood the term completely until this moment in the Dreamlands. Night literally fell. The blackness of the sky had descended, obliterating the white-and-gray light of Dreamland day and dusk like a dam bursting, dark water erasing everything in its path. Like water, it also swirled in places, whole galaxies twirling above and around us. It wasn't simply black either.

It was dark purple and navy and browns mixing and twisting so some light peeped through, but only on its own terms. Only through the wishes of the rushing, consuming night. It was, I realized with a start, the exact same night as Ny's eyes. Which, in a way, made it easier to deal with because it felt familiar. Not safe, but familiar.

Ny finding us before the flair of spark and flame lighting Ulthar became too distant made me real happy in this context, especially since I heard slithering things in the darker shadows ahead—things reminding me of monsters in my shadow world.

"What's out there?" I asked, craning my neck around the expectant face of Ny.

"Things you do not wish to encounter again. Things you'd wish to never see."

I swallowed. Yep, I was for sure happy Ny had shown up when he had.

Ny gave me a kiss on my cheek, letting loose a sigh of relief I imagined him holding since we left. He'd been worried. More worried than he'd let on when he'd told us what we had to do.

"We're safe," Gareth said, stepping up to pat Ny on the shoulder in a reassuring gesture. "Your protectors saw to it."

Ny straightened himself, and it felt like the night sky above us gathering. Looking toward the cats, he nodded at the orange leader and started a conversation in a series of mewls and chirps. Sadly, I didn't speak cat, so I couldn't follow. I did, however, take the time to look for our littlest protector and reached down to give the tiny black furball a few ear scritches as Ny wrapped up his cat debriefing.

I straightened and leaned into Gareth, letting his stiff body take some of my weight. The closeness felt nice. It also made me realize his calm aura was diminished, like it so often was when he was extra nervous or jittery. He'd said little the entire time we'd been in the Dreamlands, simply done what was necessary with his usual caution. Gareth wasn't overly talkative most times, but he did chat and occasionally joke. There were lots of reasons not to joke at the moment: Mia being kidnapped by Gareth's enemy, us entering the Dreamlands, and everyone dealing with magic crap outside our human realm. Still, thinking back on his behavior and demeanor made my gut twist.

Hell, maybe I shouldn't have been worried about Gareth and Ny's worry or issues. Maybe my sole focus should've been Mia. It was the majority of my focus, true, but Gareth and Ny were mine too. Not mine the same way Mia was mine, but mine all the same. I wanted her back, and every moment she was off having gods-know-what done to her, a part of me raged. A similar part hurt for my guys, what they had to do and how they felt about all of it. In the same way, a part hurt for Merry and Harley back in the human realm with no way of knowing what was happening here. A whole mess of people were now firmly lodged in my gut, several more than I had a few months ago when I stumbled on Starry Wisdom, and I had to navigate their feelings as well as my own. Not necessarily a bad thing. Simply what a person had to do when then came to care for people.

I took a moment to turn toward Gareth, plant my hands on his solid chest, and look up into his eyes. They were more brown than green here, and I didn't know if it was a Dreamlands thing or an inner-turmoil thing, making his hazel eyes shift their usual color.

"How you doing, big guy?"

"I'm fine."

"Fine is a cop-out. How're you really doing?"

He grumbled, then hugged me tight to his chest so my face planted in his tee. "I'm worried about every-thing. Mostly about Mia, but also you and how all of this will affect you. I'm also worried I shouldn't have come here because I might not be able to help. In fact, I might prove a hindrance at some point."

"Not likely," I muttered into his shirt before pushing away to catch his gaze. "I want you here. Need you here. Because of your knowledge and skill, yes, but also because I just plain need you right now."

A heartbeat passed before his eyes melted and warmed, and he pulled me in tight once again to kiss the top of my head. "You gut me sometimes, Randy."

"As she does us all," I heard Ny say from behind me.

I twirled around but stayed in Gareth's arms, needing to be close with him physically and sensing he might need the same. "Important cat meeting over?"

"Don't underestimate the cats of Ulthar, sweetling. They are cunning and deadly warriors."

"Does your black lion form help you relate to them or something?"

"Or something." He explained more after a beat. "We've done each other various services throughout time, and all cats have long memories. Lucky for you, because they seem to like you."

"Really?" I practically gushed. Didn't know why, but the respect of a cat always felt a little special. The respect of cat warriors felt like a gold star.

"Yes. You apparently won them over by being kind to their youngest recruit before they revealed themselves to you."

The black kitten. Who knew? Goes to show stopping to pet a cute animal has multiple benefits.

"I'm actually real happy to hear that, Ny, but we also need to chat about other things. Should we do it here or..." I let the question die as I looked around. The road was deserted, and it was full dark night, but I felt eyes on me somehow.

"You are correct, Randy. In the Dreamlands, the night has all its senses."

"The night watches us?" Gareth asked, his eyes shifting with nervous glances.

"I apologize. It's a saying here. More of a metaphor. The night itself does not literally have consciousness per se. Rather, things in the night, of the night. Predators who care little for anything but what they can catch. Some who'd even dare test a power of the Prince of the Dreamlands."

I scoffed. "Seems not too smart."

"Sometimes, sweetling, instinct wins out," he said, and his voice held enough of a growl I knew he understood what it meant to let instinct guide his way rather than reason.

A few beats of silence then Ny ushered us onto the moving shadow, which I only knew I stepped on because the texture of the ground shifted beneath my feet. "We'll go to our next destination before we discuss further." We zipped away, the night and whatever it hid closing in as the dark sky swirled overhead.

NY STOPPED US AT the top of a ridge overlooking a bay with crashing waves below. Behind us was a shack with a nearly falling in, honest-to-God thatched roof. At least, it looked like it from the outside. Inside was different, something obviously manipulated by Ny or other magic. The room was twice as big as it should've been, with strong maroon walls and a sturdy-looking ceiling with no thatching in sight. The only thing in the room was a large, comfy-looking bed that'd make a California King feel inadequate.

"I hope this will be adequate for the night."

"Better than a flimsy tent," I said with a shrug, peeling out of my jeans and jacket to climb into the bed in my tee and panties. No need to get the thing dirty. I patted the spaces beside me. "Come on then. Let's chat."

Gareth looked at Ny. He wasn't hesitating because he thought we'd be unsafe. We all could sense the wards Ny had put up. He hesitated for other reasons. DD also knew the possible score, shuddering out of sight, off to wherever it hung when it felt me and the dudes needed our privacy.

"Come on," I whined. "I'm tired, the bed is comfy, and we all need sleep. We also need to talk about the Oracle business. Why not do it in bed?"

Quirking a dark brow at Gareth, Ny sauntered over and was about to climb in before I tsked at him. "Don't get your dirty clothes on this nice, clean bed."

"Want me undressed for you, sweetling?" he asked, his voice dropping an octave.

"I want to sleep in a bed not filled with Dreamland dirt and grime," I answered, turning up my nose.

He peeled off his clothes, piece by piece, until all he had on was a pair of black boxer briefs.

"Better?"

"You may enter," I said, teasing, before I looked at Gareth. "You too, big guy."

He said nothing but stripped down to his blue plaid boxers. I took a moment to drool over my dudes before I refocused. We all sat on the bed, facing one another, when I began our story of Ulthar.

"Okay, so the Oracle was odd," I admitted to Ny, then went into detail recounting all he told us. Gareth dropped more details, about position and tone and his take on the Oracle, as I went. When we came to the end, the passing of the weird silver key, Ny stopped me.

"May I see this key?"

"Sure." I wiggled down off the bed and picked up my discarded jeans to pull it out of my tiny front pocket. "Catch," I said, throwing the thing in the air for Ny to grab. It hung there too long, hovering slowly as if stuck in anti-gravity. Ny grabbed it from its slow descent when it finally reached the bed area and studied it closely.

"What's it open?" Gareth asked him.

"A gate," Ny said, his voice deep and dark around the edges.

"What kind of gate?" I asked as I crawled back to my spot on the bed.

"The gate to the cosmos, guarded by Umr at-Tawil, a servant of my sibling Yog-Sothoth."

Gareth cursed under his breath. Seemed he knew what Ny was talking about, but I was still clueless.

"Okay. What's it mean?"

"It means, Randy..." Ny practically hissed as he clutched the key in his hand. "The Oracle gave you an object of power long thought lost. An object only spoken of in whispers, and in the Necronomicon."

"Do I have to go through this gate to get Mia back?"

Ny shook his head. "No. Impossible. Nothing living, save Yog and our sire King Azathoth, knows how one would reach the hidden gate to the outer cosmos. It's a hidden place in a hidden corner of space which, one assumes, holds many secrets. Some likely good, and some very, very bad."

"Why give Randy the silver key?" Gareth asked.

"I don't know. I've never seen it and I don't understand the Oracle's reasoning. Obviously. Not while the Book of Knowing is still missing." He threw the key back to me, and it did its weird hovering trick again before I plucked it from the air and turned to drop it in my boot. It was important enough for me to keep super close, and the tiny pocket wasn't too secure. It'd stay snug in my boot, despite the fact it might dig into my feet. I'd deal with any blisters later.

I returned to the bed for a recap and redirection. "I have a key that may or may not be useful or horrible, and a name of a mountain. Kadath. Let's focus there. Do you know where it is?"

"Yes. It's the Dreamlands home of the Earthly Gods, the ones we often call the Other Gods. The place is untouched and unknown by humans."

"Until now," I muttered.

"Until now," Ny said, a bit more firmly.

"When you say 'home of the Earthly Gods'..." Gareth asked.

"It is where the gods of Earth come, after most stop believing in them in your realm. Some take multiple forms and hold out on Earth longer, but most eventually come here, for peace and rest after they are no longer useful for humans."

Ny looked at us in turn, then closed his eyes for a beat before he continued. "If Mia is in Kadath, she was taken by one of the Other Gods. We now have a formidable opponent."

"More formidable than you?" I asked softly. I didn't want to make him upset, but we needed to know.

"If they secretly hold the Book of Knowing and can access any of its power, or spells in the Necronomicon through Mia, yes. They could well be more formidable than I currently am."

"Well, shit."

"All is not lost. Not yet. We can travel there quickly by ship. I doubt all the gods of Kadath know my plight or would side with someone attempting to wrest my power. They are here in the Dreamlands at my leisure, after all."

"So all this is ultimately some power trip by an old god who's jealous?" I asked.

"Sounds like it," Gareth replied.

"Fucking fabulous," I grumbled.

Ny inched closer, cupping my cheek in his hands. "We will retrieve your sister and all will be righted, sweetling."

"You don't know for sure. Not without your book," I said.

"I can know it here," the Prince said, thumping his hand over his chest. "Because I know you here." He then pressed his palm over my heart. "You'd tear the universe apart to get your sister back, and we'd help you, every step along the way."

I rubbed my face against his palm and nodded.

Gareth scooted closer, hesitating a moment with his hand above my knee. I nodded and his big, warm palm landed there, rubbing in large circles.

I sighed and shifted closer to both men. Ny pulled back, worry marring his beautiful face, before he said, "Randy, we need only rest here."

"I need more than rest, Ny. If you both are willing to give me more. I need to feel something other than stress and worry and pain and sadness, if only for a few minutes."

"We can help you feel," Gareth said, his voice a deep timbre shooting down my spine, right to my core.

"Maybe we all need help in this way," Ny said, and I thought of what he must be feeling, being in the home he had been ripped away from, with less power than he'd ever had. Knowing and not knowing so much when he was used to godhead. I thought of my chat with Gareth about his guilt and worry. Ny was probably right. We all needed help—a bit of a release—and maybe that was the most human thing any of us could feel in the moment, even if only two out of three of us were human. We couldn't immediately change a whole lot of real shitty things, but we could take a breather, regroup, allow desire to connect us, and create a release. Make ourselves feel alive and vital and whole for one shiny moment in time.

Ny grabbed the back of my neck and dragged me toward him until our mouths met in a soft, deep kiss. His tongue coaxed and caressed, its lush roughness causing goose bumps to spread across my body. He dropped his hand and I pulled back, turning to meet Gareth for a kiss as well, his sweet, gentle mouth different but no less affecting.

When we came up for air, Ny tugged the hem of my tee up and threw the thing to the floor, exposing my breasts to their hungry gazes. Neither spoke. Both moved in unison, each latching on, the feeling similar yet different. Each tongue and mouth and suction unique but familiar.

I cried out from the sensation and felt Ny's satisfied chuckle against my nipple before he popped off to say, "Like that, sweetling?"

I was about to answer when Gareth gave a quick bite to my other nipple, causing lust to zing up my body and my back to arch with pleasure.

"I see you do," he purred, pushing my back to the bed.

Gareth followed, not losing his grip on my nipple, as Ny traced kisses down my full belly and over my wide hips, heading right toward the tuft of curls between my thighs. Those thighs shook with want as he palmed each, pushing them open.

He stared at my damp curls, sniffed deep, and murmured, "So lovely," with his eyes closed in bliss. He dove in, his purring, scratchy tongue hitting my clit instantly. I sucked in a breath then let out a long, slow groan of deep pleasure. Ny was so damn good at this, I was more than happy to lie back and take the pleasure he gave.

Gareth lifted up and cupped my face, his stare intense on me. "You look so fucking good like this, spread out for us."

Ny's tongue hit a pace a hair shy of punishing, and my body shook involuntarily in response. Gareth continued to stare at me as one hand traveled down his body, over his tasty, muscled form and right to his hips. He pumped those hips, and I knew what he was doing.

"Let me watch," I whispered, pulling myself up on my elbows to get a better look at my big guy.

He didn't answer, just did as I asked and rose to sitting, moving to palm one of my tits as his other hand gripped his hard length tight. He gave a sharp tug and bit back a moan. I echoed the sentiment and lost focus for a moment, what I saw of Gareth and what Ny's tongue was doing to me almost too much. Too much in the most delicious way. My head fell back between my shoulder blades and though it was much quicker than usual for me, my orgasm barreled down my body. My limbs shook, my head lolled, and I cried out in surprise and satisfaction as Ny licked me to completion.

The Prince slid up my body, his hot flesh heating my own as it moved over me. He rose on one arm and cocked his head toward Gareth, who was still pumping his dick beside me. He smiled, chucked Gareth on the chin as if happy to see the sight too, then focused those starry-space eyes right on my face. "I need you," he said, his soft voice ringing through the lust still clouding my brain, straight through the magic already pouring out around us.

"You have me." I looped my arms around his neck, brought his mouth to mine so I could taste our passion on his talented tongue, and urged him on with my moans and mewls.

I felt him notch at my entrance half a beat before he eased himself into me, a slow, steady thrust ending only when his entire length was buried deep inside me. His eyes had their black glow. I was sure mine were all magic too. None of it mattered. What mattered was the feeling, the oblivion, the release every single one of us needed.

"Gareth." I called to him as I took one arm from Ny and reached for the mage. He scooted closer, his breath coming out in pants matching the rhythm of his hand. "I want you close."

He said nothing and moved closer as I asked, close enough to dip down and give me a jolting kiss before pulling up and saying, "Fuck her."

Ny obliged, starting close before reaching up, up, up into a hard and steady pace. The sound of our flesh hitting was echoed by Gareth's strokes on his own flesh, and we became a trio of moans, groans, and sweaty skin.

Nothing mattered in the moment, only the shiny release we all saw at the end of a dark tunnel. We rose together, higher and higher, until Ny snaked a hand between us and flicked my clit a few times in a row, sending me spiraling right into the light. He fell sooner after, his pumping hips jerking with his orgasm. Gareth's warm release splashed on my chest, and I turned in time to see the glorious tail end: his hand shaking as he came on me, his back arched slightly, his face a strain of pleasure, and his muscled form tight, then relax.

I sank into the post-release glow and the swirl of magic, the new space and shadow cloud with shots of green. Our magic we made all together. Ny rolled off of me to scoot to the edge of the bed and grab his pants. In the meantime, Gareth used the outside of his blue boxers to wipe my breasts. "Sorry," he muttered.

"No worries," I said, stretching above him. I had worries, of course, but not about this or anything he'd done. It all felt too good and had been just what I needed to relax a touch, get out of my own head for a few marvelous minutes.

Gareth threw the now-soiled boxers off the bed and stayed naked, pulling me to his chest and giving a gentle kiss to the top of my head. We both lay back, snuggled, and Ny fiddled with the magic-holding watch.

"Gareth, please sit up a moment," he called. He complied and Ny twirled his fingers in a blur of intricate patterns before reaching out to Gareth's forearms. The sigils flared as they were topped off with power. Ny swirled the rest down into the pocket watch, which he closed with a loud click.

"Here you are, friend. A reserve if you should need it." Ny handed Gareth the pocket watch to keep, but the mage threw it on top of his heap of clothes on the floor and immediately lay back down to snuggle close once again.

Ny moved to my other side, wrapping his hand around my belly and giving a squeeze. "Now. Rest."

I let out a loud yawn. "Yep, but not because you demand it or anything."

I felt his smile, heard it as he said, "Of course not, sweetling."

Gareth also chuckled in my ear, sounding sleepy himself. As Ny had pointed out before, we all needed rest.

"Night," I said, turning my head right, then left to give each man a quick peck on the chest.

"Good night, Randy."

"Sleep well, sweetling."

I burrowed in deep between the two, feeling safe and sleepy and more relaxed than I had in the entire journey. As I drifted off to sleep, I thought of the warmth all around me and the luck I had to have these two men at my side to help me out however I needed.

Fifteen

I HAD TO PEE so bad, it was a minor miracle I didn't have an accident as I shimmied back into my pants and quickly pulled on my boots. The little shack had a great bed, but Ny hadn't considered the human need for a toilet in the middle of the night. Outside it was. DD had popped back up sometime while I slept, and it hovered, my tiny shadow guard in the night.

I'd camped enough to know to pop a squat close to the shack, but I circled to the back and several yards away. I did my business, shook myself as best I could, and was fastening my jeans back when I heard a swishing sound, like wings. Giant wings. It was then I remembered Ny's warnings about what lurked in the dark of the Dreamlands, but it was already too late.

I felt claws dig into my shoulders and lift me off the ground with a punishing grip. I screamed as the thing maneuvered me in midair so I was in its arms, held tight by four sets of razor-sharp claws digging into flesh through my tee and jeans. I thrashed, trying to get free, but I felt myself rising in the air impossibly fast, each millisecond a wing beat up, up, up, until the shack hovered below an impossible length below. Terrified I'd fall to my death, I stopped squirming and called DD to me. I screamed for Ny and it zipped off, ready to tell the Outer God I'd been taken. I was, again, a little late. It hurried off to help in some way, but I couldn't even see the shack anymore and had no idea where I was. Hopefully DD would return after telling the dudes, and Ny and Gareth could get to me quick. Not much else I could do in the situation. Any magic I'd have access to would likely result in falls and splats.

After resigning myself to wait for rescue, I finally looked at the thing gripping me tight, taking me away to gods-knew-where in the swirl of night. It was something straight out of nightmares yet different from the rolling, slippery, multi-eyed nightmare creatures I'd encountered before. First, there were wings—big, leathery batlike wings with intricate bone structure protruding in incongruent spots and a fleshy looking membrane instead of feathers or whatnot. The wings sprung from its back, so it had four other limbs, all tipped in many-fingered claws. Those claws weren't nail based or talons but really the fingers or digits themselves, tapering into sharp points. I thought of the forelimbs as arms and the back limbs as legs, but nothing in the anatomy, shape, or structure made it immediately similar to my own body. Human-world bodies were just all I had in mind to comprehend the thing.

The entire thing, like the fingers, was impossibly thin. So thin I worried it'd drop me because I likely had a whole lot of weight on it. In the night it was hard to tell, but it seemed a sickly gray color with a face horribly filled with nothing. Literally nothing. A vortex of a black hole. A total blankness. A swirl of matching night with no beginning or end only nothing, topped with big curling horns coming from its head. All in all, nightmare fuel.

Then, the damn thing started tickling me, which may at first have sounded funny but definitely was not. I'd never liked tickling. There was always too much questionable consent for me, and I wasn't super ticklish, so even under normal circumstances, it was a weird touchy thing I didn't appreciate. It dug its long, sharp fingers into my ribs and armpits, making me nearly vomit with disgust instead of laugh, while I became more and more sure my wiggling would make the thing drop me from the sky at any moment.

I started hyperventilating as we went farther and farther into the sky, where I assumed the air was thinner even in the Dreamlands. I panicked—screamed, thrashed, and cursed—as the thing climbed the sky and tickled me until I blacked out from the weird horror of the situation.

Eventually I came to, thanks to DD giving soft taps to my cheek, but I couldn't say how long I had been out. Could've been minutes or hours. It was still night, and I was still flying high with the gray monster. DD sent reassurance down our line, and I knew it'd told Ny and Gareth what happened. Didn't know where the hell they were, but they'd get there. They'd come for me no matter what, which was a good thing I clung to in my mind.

The other good thing was it'd stopped tickling me, so I wasn't dodging creepy-ass fingers anymore. The not-so-good thing was it felt like we were descending, which meant we might land somewhere, which meant I could be anywhere in the Dreamlands and anything could happen next.

I panicked again. Screamed and thrashed more. Then, a familiar sound blared in my mind. The sound of an old telephone. I stilled, went inward, reached for the old wall phone in my head connecting me to Merry and answered.

"Are you okay?" she screamed down the line. Her voice sounded distant, crackly. Our connection was like a cell phone going through a tunnel, but it was there, and it gave me courage and strength to hear her voice.

"I will be. Don't worry. And we know where Mia is now, so we'll have her back soon."

A shuddering cry of worry and joy came down the line, then a dial tone. The call hadn't lasted long, but it had done the trick. It reminded me who I was, who I needed to be to protect the people I loved.

I steeled myself, found my center like Harley had taught me so long ago, and tried to ignore all the super scary things about the creature who'd flown me somewhere far away from Ny and Gareth. I waited, patiently, until I felt us slow, and turned my eye toward the ground now creeping closer and closer.

There wasn't much to see. Night swallowed most details. I did see something darker, larger. We got closer and I made it out: a pit. The thing was flying right down into a massive pit in the ground, where it swooped in, not even slowing much. It did, however, skim closer to the ground as it tried to navigate the enclosed landscape. We flew so close, I wasn't afraid of falling to my death any longer. It was a chance, the only one I'd had since the thing swooped down on me, and I took it.

With a blink of thought, I asked DD to bubble out around me, creating a barrier between me and the thing. It ballooned in an instant, creating a small force field around my body and dislodging the flying creature in its wake. The thing screeched, an inhuman sound that pierced my eardrums and left me crying out in pain. The impact on the ground, a thump, and the skidding across hard-packed soil also didn't help. Lucky for me, the thing hit as hard and hadn't braced for impact like I had. It smacked right into a small outcropping of rocks embedded in the dirt, letting out a deep grunt as it hit. I scrambled to my feet as quickly as possible and reached for my spear almost on instinct. Crouched in a fighting stance, I faced the gray, long-fingered, weird ass tickle monster, ready to fight.

Apparently I didn't need to, not yet anyway, because it wasn't moving a muscle. I breathed deep, trying to calm my racing heart and think through the mess I was in, when I heard something like a soft growl behind me. I whirled, DD's bubble shield in place and my spear raised in defense, and found sets of glowing eyes slinking toward me in the gloom of the pit. Something else held a magical light of some kind. It moved toward me slowly, examining me as it came closer and closer.

I felt the circle tightening, surrounding... closing in all around me. The one with light became clearer, and I saw a canine creatures moving on crouched legs like hunched-over people. They had claws and teeth and smattering of fur around. Their long snouts reminded me of Doberman pinschers, but much bigger and scarier. In fact, the more I saw of them in the low light, the more they looked like freaking werewolves with larger heads and more pointed muzzles. More nightmare fuel, but somehow less nightmarish because they looked like the regular old monsters humans had invented centuries ago. Then I thought these things might actually be where werewolf myths had come from, and the idea made them scary again.

I assumed the one holding the ball of magical, pulsing light in their upturned paw was the leader. It gave a low snarl, stepped within about twenty feet of me, and turned its nose up for a deep sniff. It was scenting me, probably wondering if I smelled like a tasty treat. Whatever it was I smelled like made the thing stop cold and dead, like preternaturally unmoving. Its eyes bulged, its head dipped in a weird submissive posture, and the entire line took several too-quick, too-large steps back, giving me room. The light wavered as the creature actually went down on its wrong-way knees and kneeled in front of me in a bow. The circle, one by one, was bowing low to me.

I thought they had to be scenting Ny on me. We'd just had sex, and Ny had assured me earlier Mia was safe because she simply wore his scent on his vest. I had much more of his scent covering me. I scrambled to my feet and used as close to Ny's flippant, imperious tone as I could muster. "You're smart to stay back. Prince Nyarlathotep would not wish me harmed. He would be very displeased."

A shiver went through the crowd, and they all backed up another half step in unison, giving me even more space. The leader made a series of sounds I took as some form of instruction, and several of the things peeled off from the group and scurried toward the winged creature, still out cold behind me. The contingent stayed as far from me as possible as it worked, securing the thing with some type of rope and hauling it off into the deeper, darker recesses of the pit. At least the tickle monster was gone. The others weren't going anywhere, but they kept their distance. I had no clue what they were, where I was, or anything else, really. Fight or flight both seemed like bad ideas, given my complete lack of info, so I decided, as long as they stayed away, I'd stay put and wait it out. I trusted Ny and Gareth to come for me. I wasn't exactly someone who needed rescuing on a regular basis, but sometimes a little rescuing was in order given the circumstances.

As I waited, I paced. I worried. I literally kicked rocks. I reassured DD, who was still hovering as a protective bubble around me, but it was really more about hearing my own voice and reassuring myself. Eventually, white light peeked around the edges of night I could see from of the mouth of the pit and guessed Dreamland morning approached. Not long after, I felt a crackle of dark power zing across my skin, then dip and pull at my magical thrum inside, and I smiled my own catlike smile at the still-gathered things around me. Shit was about to go down for them, and I was about to be rescued. Marvelous.

In moments, Ny and Gareth swooped in on the tail of a shadow, Ny's power sizzling in the air all around him. Gareth's sigils glowed, heavy and dark like a licking flame up his tatted arms. DD dropped only when Ny stepped onto the mound. He slammed into me, his hands on my face.

"Randy, are you hurt?" he growled in his echoing Outer God voice.

"Not physically, but it's been a hell of a night."

Gareth hugged into my side, feeling my solidness and rightness for himself before he blew out a harsh breath.

Ny turned and screamed, "Bring me the night gaunt who thought my sweeting game," stomping toward the circled creatures with anger and malice written on his face.

The leader bowed, snapped impossible fingers, and a group brought the gray-winged creature up for Ny. It had awakened at some point and was not happy to be held captive, struggling every step of the way. More grunts and growls sounded from the werewolf things before they threw the winged creature at Ny's feet. He reached out a hand, twisting the void in the thing's face as it convulsed, suspended in the air. It didn't make a sound, but somehow, I felt like it let out a silent scream of agony. Maybe it was all in my mind. It wrenched and twisted in obvious pain for a full minute before Ny gave a guttural scream of rage, his eyes deadly space. He reached for the thing's head and ripped it clear off its body, flinging it to the side as he dropped the dead creature at his feet.

I gasped, but it was a gasp of surprise rather than judgment. Ny looked at me, pain and worry on his face, but I scuttled down the mound and gave him a big hug of thanks. I didn't know what it said about me, being able to dismiss the killing of the creature so quickly, but I did. It had hurt me, but more importantly, Ny's haunted eyes told me without words it was what he needed to do for both of us. Gareth's stony exterior showed no judgment either. I guessed no one was too picky about killing when people we cared about were threatened.

Ny let me hold him for several beats before he put me in Gareth's arms and gave harsh demands in the growly, guttural language of the werewolf creatures of the pit. We humans stayed quiet until I heard a garbled, jumbled version of "Necronomicon" and "girl" followed by a clearly stated name in English: Richard Pickman.

"What?" I shouted, stepping closer to the light-holding leader. It seemed afraid of me and shuffled back quickly at my approach.

Ny stopped it with an outstretched hand and commanded it with a motion to come closer. "They speak some English, but little. I take it you picked up the last few parts?"

"Yeah. What are they saying?" I eyed them warily, and Ny tilted his head toward me.

"They are far too hesitant to attempt to cause you any harm, Randy."

"Because you ripped the thing's head off in front of them."

Ny crinkled his brow and said, "No, because they scented your power, then mine. I'm not completely fluent in their language, only passable, but it sounds like they're going on about you and the moon."

No idea what me or the moon had to do with anything, but I had more pressing concerns. "What'd they say about Mia?"

"A great deal, much of it very good for your sister and us." He spoke with them for a few more moments. They bowed to him—and to me for some reason—and shuffled back step by step until they disappeared into the dark of the deep pit.

"Come. We must travel back toward the sea and Dylath-Leen. We'll discuss what transpired here along the way."

I didn't argue. I knew Ny'd tell us everything. The sooner I got out of this infernal pit, the better.

Sixteen

WE FLITTED ON A shadow across shadows, and Gareth and I acted like it was no big deal. For me, it felt more and more real. It was an extension of the many different types of shadow powers I'd revealed in the past six months. I felt it in my thrum, the connection and pull of the shadow moving us along, so it became ho-hum in no time. I didn't know how Gareth had gotten used to it so quickly or if he was just pretending to be. Either way, it was a cozy setting—me, Ny, and Gareth huddled together in a loose circle with our heads bent down to chat. The shadow zipped us this way and that through the Dreamlands, taking us toward some seaport named Dylath-Leen, which was closer to the shack from the previous night.

I told them they didn't need to apologize or explain why they hadn't caught up with me until dawn, but they needed to explain anyway. DD had woken them, something my screams hadn't been able to do inside the enchanted room, and Gareth cast a solid tracking spell after Ny figured out that a night gaunt, one of those creeping predators in the dark of the Dreamlands, had snatched me up with no purpose other than food. I didn't like the idea I'd nearly been the meal for some giant, winged tickle monster, but I'd made it out, so I didn't press for more info about night gaunts in general. There was already too much info for me to press about.

They'd figured out what had happened quickly, but they'd had a transportation issue, which was why it had taken so long to get to me. It was night, and they couldn't track and travel via shadow too well because night was dark and all that and darkness basically made actual cast shadows few and far between, and apparently shadow hopping as a mode of transport is real specific and finicky. All it meant was it frustratingly slow going for them to reach me. Ny'd been beyond angry when they'd reached me, mainly because it was near dawn, and night gaunts liked to have a big meal before they slept for the day. It had landed in the pit to find a place to eat and rest. It had been bad luck for it that I'd reacted and there'd been other creatures there lurking in the dark.

My dudes felt guilty it had taken so long to catch up with me, but I told them they reached me, so it didn't matter. I'd survived. Everything else was secondary to the fact I had heard Mia's name brought up, so as soon as we cleared a few shadows outside the space, I pressed Ny to spill what they'd said.

"The ghouls did not see Mia. Not all of them, at least. The pack leader you encountered, Fex, had run into a different ghoul, from another pack, so was tracking Mia. His name is Richard Pickman, and I know him well. He will find her, protect her as best he can until we catch up with them."

"How did this Pickman start tracking her in the first place?" Gareth asked.

"He's half human, half ghoul. Was once a fairly distinguished painter in Boston at the turn of the twentieth century, until his more ghoulish traits made him flee the human realm. I knew him in both realms, was a friend to him in each. I can't exactly detail his motivations, but I can make some assumptions based on what I know of him, and I believe our hope—the hope my vest would offer some protection—was realized with Rich."

"What are ghouls?" I asked, needing to know who was tracking my sister.

"Ghouls are all, to some degree, already part human and part Dreamlander," Gareth said. "I've encountered many, in various degrees in and out of transformation in my time in the occult world. Like people, like everyone, they can be good or bad."

I closed my eyes and inwardly groaned to myself. Ny'd given me a nice set down about assumptions I might have made in the dark pit, and he could've been a lot snippier about it. I'd deserve it for being a bit of an ass. Reminders to not judge books by covers were always necessary, even in weird circumstances or new realms. "Sorry," I grumbled toward Ny, hugging myself. "They look scary and all werewolf-like, and I just needed to know, you know?"

Ny waved his hand in the air, as if taking my rudeness in stride, and said, "Rich is a friend. Not only this, he is a powerful ghoul with exceptional tracking skills. He will help Mia escape if he can, will work to keep her in his sights and safe if he cannot. I trust this."

"And I trust you," I said, blowing out a breath and trying to leech away some of the worry, "so I'll trust your friend too. He's not a royal or anything, right?" The line from the Oracle was stuck in my mind, and I wanted to make sure I wasn't trusting some other royal.

"There are no ghoul royals. They govern by pack structure, with established leaders, but mostly it is mutual aid." Gareth always had the facts.

"The royals the Oracle mentioned will be the gods we'll meet on Kadath. They live by a more hierarchical structure, including royal titles in some cases. Too much to get into now, and not exceedingly important. I no longer have true friends in their ranks, so I would say none are completely trustworthy, even if many have been allies in the past."

"You had friends who were gods once?" Gareth asked.

"Yes. Long ago." Ny didn't continue, and I elbowed Gareth to make sure he didn't press. There was history there, and Ny would let us know if we needed to or if he felt comfortable sharing. We didn't need to drag sad times out of him. We were already in enough trouble without clouding everyone with stories of our sordid pasts.

Ny turned to look at me, appearing to have been reminded of something, and said, "Are you not interested in why the ghouls bowed to you?"

"No."

Gareth said, "Randy..."

"Doesn't matter. Unless it's something we can figure out soon, or it's something we know for certain would give us a better chance of getting Mia back more quickly, then it's not worth our brain power. We need to focus on immediate things like how the hell we're going to get to Kadath."

"We're going to sail right into its harbor, with as much fanfare as possible," Ny said, all blasé, and I stared at him, dumbfounded. I guessed there was no more sneaking about then.

WE REACHED DYLATH-LEEN FROM above about midday. The bright-white sky capped a deep black sea encasing small, neatly outlined city streets. It was a port, similar to most port towns in the human realm. It looked more industrial than Ulthar, more like a place where markets and commerce and trade were king.

Ny swooped into the city without hesitation. He didn't hide his presence but didn't highlight it either. Mostly, he went about his business efficiently. As Prince of the Dreamlands, the buzz of his arrival traveled quick as hell.

He met with some people at a shipping house while Gareth and I waited outside. The two-story stacked-stone building faced a large dock full of motions, smells, and briny tastes. The smell and taste of saltwater was familiar to my palate–fresh and alkaline and slightly fishy. Flashes of other things tingled my nose and tastebuds, namely a sweet tang I couldn't describe but sat heavy in my nose and on my tongue like it wanted to stay a while. Then, the sight and smell of people pushed through.

Ny didn't stay in the building long, but every minute brought more and more people. A crowd of all sorts of creatures gathered, a respectful distance away, and stood muttering among themselves. I heard a few words here and there, making me realize they were waiting for Ny to emerge. They wanted to see him for themselves.

"It's weird," I said quietly.

"He's their Prince," Gareth replied.

I eyed the crowd, felt their sense of awe and anticipation, and maybe it was the first time I really understood what Ny being Prince meant beyond his major magical heft. It was a leadership position, a responsibility. Something like what I felt for Mia and Merry as eldest sister but a million times bigger while also being less personal. He'd had it all his infinite life, and he wore magical and political power so well, I rarely remembered what he was. It was right for Harley to remind me, for Gareth to point it out, because it was right for these people to want to feel close to someone who had a very real effect on their lives in so many ways I'd never even considered.

Ny emerged into the whiteness of day and moved toward us after a passing glance at the crowd. Before anything else, he asked "Are you well? Overwhelmed?"

"No, Ny. Do what you need to do," Gareth said, taking my hand as I smiled encouragement at our Prince.

He dipped his head, turned, and he was on in an instant. Slightly distant but kind. Shaking hands, waving, chatting. It lasted maybe thirty minutes, and I wasn't mad about the delay. We'd likely had to wait for a ship regardless. Ny using the time to talk and give out small smiles was important for all these people.

When he'd managed to wave the crowd off, he came back and said, "It won't be like this the rest of the time we're in Dylath-Leen. My people generally give me a good berth once I've interacted with a larger crowd in any given place."

I kissed his cheek without saying anything, and he smiled his slow, sexy cat smile down at me. "I am glad my princely duties make you sweet, my Randy."

"Don't count on it lasting." I moved away from him before I got ensnared too much by his mouth and those eyes. "What's the plan?"

"The plan, sweetling, is to board a black ship and sail straight to Kadath. We will leave with the tide and should arrive at the mount tomorrow morning."

"I thought there was going to be pomp and circumstance, My Prince," I said, teasing him.

"Oh, there will be," he replied. "You need to see the black ship to understand."

HE WAS RIGHT. I'D imagined a simple ship painted black. Nope. Not even close. It was something out of a goth sailor fever dream. The thing was a sailboat, but like an old timey one humans used to use before steam and gas took over shipping. It was also massive, a floating mountain. At the very least, a huge floating hill. The boat was so big, it blotted out the whiteness of the day, almost siphoning the white light away and turning everything to night. Except it didn't have the Dreamland night-sky swirls. It was a void—a void moving so fast it loomed in front of us quickly, moving from horizon to dock in less than ten minutes.

"Is that thing made from the same wood as the black church?" I asked, my stomach churning at the possibility when it was nearly on top of us.

"It is, love, but I swear, you have nothing to fear while on board. The wood itself is neutral in power. Starry Wisdom used it to do horrible things. These sailors use it to cut through the sea and trade across my realm. You'll feel the difference when you get close to it."

I still gave the thing side-eye, until I felt the soft ebb and flow of it, so tranquil and easy. So unlike the creepy feel of the black church. It made me far less hesitant to get on board the boat. The need to get to Mia as fast as possible also helped.

The sailors onboard worked hard, paying little attention to us except to give small smiles or waves or grunts of greeting. Fine by me. They seemed like busy, competent people I didn't need to bother because they were doing us a solid.

"The gods will see us coming in this," Gareth said.

"We want them to see us," Ny said. "No one approaches Kadath without leave from the gods or me, and even fewer can command a ride on a black ship. They will make assumptions I want them to make and act accordingly. I don't plan for us to hide. If we want to figure out who holds Mia, we must show ourselves—use my position and their deference to needle out answers."

"Hide in plain sight," I said.

"A solid plan," Gareth said, his big arms crossed in his thinking stance. "What should we expect?"

"The ship will be greeted by a god, most likely the Messengers. Then we will be taken to the Palace of the Gods. We'll have a few moments to ourselves, but a formal greeting will be required, so we must attend the throne room. A dinner, dance, or similar gathering will be called. There we may be able to interact more freely with the gods and get their measure."

"This whole time, you'll act like their princely lord, and we'll do... what?" I asked.

"You'll act like my current human companions. Most know I have a proclivity for humans when in my human form and will not question it, even if your appearance in Kadath will mean welcoming humans in their palace, something they have not done in centuries. Man of the ex-gods are not known to think highly of human company, which means this plan has the joint benefit of making you untouchable while also causing many in their rank and file to think you beneath their notice completely."

All of it sounded smart, effective, and time-consuming in the way most spy work probably always was. I bit the inside of my cheek, nervous about what I was about to confess. "I don't know how long I can hold out, knowing Mia is there somewhere and not being able to bust down the doors and demand to see her."

"I know, lovely," Ny said in a reassuring voice. "We will work as quickly as possible, but I promise you, if we have not found Mia within a day of landing, we will switch tactics."

"Fair enough," I said, taking a minute to look out over the deck of the massive, swiftly moving vessel. The black waves crashed ahead in a troubled sea, but the boat was steady. Sturdy. Unwavering. Like we had to be. I reminded myself of this, reached out to grab hands with my guys, and tried to find a little extra steadiness there because I knew I would. Wherever and whenever I reached for them.

Seventeen

THE MOUNTAIN ROSE OUT of the churning, black seawater, towering so high into the sky a curtain of mist or fog obscured the top like the giant Stonehenge place in the in-between. "Kadath," Ny said.

"No shit," I said with a snort. As if Gareth and I couldn't guess the big-ass mountain would be the thing we were headed toward.

Ny cut eyes to me. "Sweetling, I love your smart mouth. In all ways. I truly do. Yet, it is in our best interest not to allow it free rein when we reach the mount."

I swallowed hard and nodded. He was right, of course. We'd made a plan, one to hopefully get Mia safely away, and I needed to stick to the plan. At least, stick to it until we had no choice but to deviate from it. Gods help us all, literally, if we had to deviate from it.

The giant ship eased into a small harbor, what would be an impossible task for many but coming off as easy-peasy to the sailors of the black ship. As we approached the dock, I saw part of the fanfare Ny had referenced earlier. Large colored banners, glittering metal, and feathers stood out from the worn wood of the pier, covering it so much, I could barely see specks of the black-wood-constructed dock peeking through. From shore to drop, the dock was a vivid welcome, a kaleidoscope of flowing color to greet our monochromatic ship. All of it ruffled in a breeze that wasn't actually breezing; magic fueled the pretty ebb and flow of color greeting us.

Lining each side were stone-still people, which as I got closer, looked like actual stone, gray and shiny as the sleek stone of the gates of Ulthar and the Oracle's place. Hell, maybe they were stone. There weren't supposed to be a whole lot of people here. No human people here anyway.

In the middle of lines of stone soldiers stood two tall figures. They were dressed in long, golden robes tied neatly at the waist with simple cord or rope. Their heads were topped with high, curving hats made of heavy gold, forming an almost tulip-like shape. It started wider at the base, flared out in the middle, and tapered to a rounded end high above their heads. Their heads were high too. We were still far away, given the size of the ship we were on, but they looked big. Tall and wide with clear muscle. They were muscle in more than one sense. No one needed to tell me these were the Messengers. If gods could choose who represented them, these two identical, intimidating figures would be the clear choice.

Ny breezed off the ship as soon as the way was cleared. Gareth and I followed a step behind, having already discussed letting Ny take the lead whenever we moved into new spaces on Kadath. He would be expected to be a step ahead. We wanted to work with the expected so we could slyly do the unexpected stuff we needed.

The two muscled men, who up close looked close to seven feet tall with arms bigger than my own ample thighs, each lowered to a knee as soon as Ny appeared. Good thing, because the power wafting off them slammed into my body, making me stutter in my step. It was a hell of a lot of power, and it made my own magic stir in my gut. Gareth shot a hand out to steady me, and I saw he looked a little wobbly as well. Us humans weren't used to the godly power business.

"Rise, Gupan and Ugar," Ny instructed in what I'd come to think of in my mind as his Prince Nyarlathotep voice: cold, distant, and imperious, with a bit of a sneer and a joke at the listener's expense.

The giant dudes came up smoothly and only then did I notice the beauty of both. They were twins, each an exact replica of the other. I doubted I'd ever be able to tell them apart. Their eyes were the color of sand, a striking light brown I'd never seen in eyes before. The thick, bushy lines of their black eyebrows contrasted the color. Their faces were smooth, hairless, the skin a shade darker than their eyes and utterly flawless. Their large mouths and pink lips were hard lines I couldn't read. Above everything else, they radiated power. Like the power Ny had, but unfamiliar. Not based in shadows, I knew. Not something I should automatically trust. My own magic rose in defense as DD sat still yet tense on my shoulder. I tamped it down, the instinct to meet their magic with my own. If I couldn't get past the guards, there was no way I was going to find Mia, so I made myself look as aloof and bored as possible while I tried to calm my magic. It was an odd feeling, my magic being defensive without me calling it forward, but I chalked it up to new-place-and-people jitters.

"Prince of Dreamlands, a pleasure to see you once again. It has been long since you graced us with your presence. We welcome you to Kadath, as always," one of the two, the one of the right, said, his eyes downcast as he spoke.

The one on the left looked beyond Ny, to me and Gareth, eyeing us up and down, and I felt those sandy eyes could look right through us. Ny's plan to come as we were, without too many lies, made even more sense now. These two could see lies a mile away, their eyes trained for such things. I definitely didn't want to lie to them. I also didn't want to look away or back down. I had always been confident and a bit mouthy, but the way I was feeling was ridiculous. Looking at these two made me want to smack them around, even though everything in my brain told me such a thing wasn't possible for a lowly human like myself. The gods in front of me made human-me quake, more than Ny ever had because he'd been connected to me from the jump. The magic in me, however, was aching for a fight.

"Yes. Yes. I assume all know of my arrival." There was no question in his voice, only command.

"Yes, Prince Nyarlathotep. All are gathering in the Great Hall to attend you immediately."

"Good." Ny sniffed. He gestured behind himself, at us. "This is Gareth and Randy, my current companions. They are to be allowed entrance and access as I am."

A muscle in the left one's jaw twitched, but both bowed their head, and the one on the right said in his smooth baritone, "Of course, Your Grace. If you and your companions would like, we can journey to the Palace immediately. However, as they are human, we will need to climb Kadath, which will take longer than usual. Will that be satisfactory, My Prince?"

Ny's answer was to slide past the two. We followed close behind. For a second, I worried we'd literally have to climb Kadath like some Everest expedition, but Ny stepped onto a platform affixed to the stony mountain side, and I saw an intricate network of chains and tracks and other mechanical things rising above us. Even gods needed goods delivered, I supposed, so it made sense they'd have some way to get stuff up they couldn't magic there for whatever reason.

Gupan and Ugar filed on after our trio, then pulled several levers stuck in the floor of the platform, and we began to rise at a surprising speed. I stumbled a bit, being the klutz I am, and instinctively grabbed out for my closest guy, which happened to be Ny. I gripped his side from behind, using him as an anchor to keep me from falling. The twin who didn't talk stared at my hand a beat before he caught my eye. He cocked his head in thought, and I felt like both hunter and prey—human-me not wanting any part of tangling with a god who looked like a pro wrestler, while magic-me screamed to stomp the floor with him. I leaned into Gareth as I squeezed Ny's side, finding a little calm pouring out of the mage despite his own nervousness and sharp-eyed stare at the twin deities in front of us.

"Is there a problem?" Ny drawled, no hint of his affectionate purr. It was all echoing power and growl directed at the twins.

Both gods immediately averted their eyes, and the talking one said, "No, Your Grace. Forgive us. It has simply been many, many centuries since we have personally seen humans from the human realm."

Ny made a humming noise which was able to sound both dismissive and aggressive at the same time. Impressive, really. Gareth and I made no sounds. Only stood as still as we could behind our Outer God as we swiftly rose up, up, up into the mists ringing the peak of Kadath. Toward the Dreamlands home of the Other Gods.

THE REST OF THE ride was quick and silent, except for the gasp I hadn't been able to keep in when we'd broken through the layer of mist and I'd first seen the Palace of the Gods looming at the very tip-top of the mountain. It wasn't exactly right to describe it as sitting there. More like it was built into the top of the mountain—a large, stone fortress with curling spires at impossible heights and angles, and bright, waving banners positioned around the structure. Opulently furnished balconies with curtains glittering like jewels were dotted all across the facade. Giant, barred gates lay ahead of us, lined with dozens more stone-statue guards we moved past to enter.

No one said anything, and I followed the lead, keeping my head down. Anyone within the Palace who moved or spoke muttered groveling words to Ny as he breezed past the tall gates, for all intents and purposes knowing exactly where he belonged. We hooked a right at a massive black-marbled entrance and took a set of winding stairs up several flights before coming to a locked pair of wide doors. Ny waved a hand and shadows unfurled from the edges of the slightly darkened hallway to creep through the doors and let us inside.

The doors swung open on their own, showing an extravagant set of rooms. A small throne was on a dais, flanked by settees someone could've lifted straight from an old-school film about the Greeks or Romans. The same black marble from the entry covered the floor here, leading us from the official-looking sitting area down a few steps into a truly decadent boudoir.

I'd never in my life used the term boudoir, but this definitely was one. Silk lined the walls. The lighting was low and sexy. The sparse furniture in the room was constructed from dark-brown wood polished to a high shine. The bed, a large square, took up an absurd amount of space, enough for ten people to pile on comfortably. It was an orgy bed, and part of me pulled back from the thought and stuffed it in the back of my mind where I'd never have to think about the things Ny did in such a bed before I'd come along. I knew who and what he was, and I had no official claim to him beyond the idea I knew he was mine. I didn't need to turn into a crazy person who suddenly cared about what a person I had no claim on did prior to our time together.

I had opened my mouth to crack some joke, mainly to make myself feel better, when Ny twirled and placed a finger to his lips before I could make a sound. Startled, I looked around, waiting to find something there with us. Before I saw much else, beyond the orgy bed and the royal meeting chamber or whatever, Ny snapped his fingers and dark descended. Shadows, actually. Big, thick, swirling shadows pulled from the edges of the ceiling to shroud us in a bubble not unlike the protective bubble shield DD did for me sometimes. It reminded me of my little friend, and I sent it a silent feeling of warmth and appreciation down whatever our bond was. I knew it got it when it gave a soft bounce on my shoulder at my unspoken praise. I was sure I'd need DD here soon enough, so I was happy it stayed calm but sharp there.

"We must be careful how we speak in the Palace," Ny said in reference to the shadow bubble he'd pulled down on us. "We can speak freely only after certain precautions."

Gareth nodded, his arms crossed and feet planted in his serious-big-guy mode. "We have a day of stealth, as you promised Randy. How will we use it?"

"We will present ourselves to the gods in the Great Hall in minutes, after provisions are presented to us. It is a formal affair, one I must attend to whenever I come here. It will also give all of us time to consider initial reactions and feelings. I will then demand time alone in the libraries, where we may find useful information, but time there will be limited. We will be required to attend some formal event this evening, whatever they can throw together on short notice. Likely a ball, which is in our favor. During a ball we can mingle, talk, feel out more individuals in this place. Then, late in the night, after the ball, we use the info we gathered to rescue Mia."

"How do you know we'll find her so quick?" I asked, wanting to believe it but needing more hope.

"Because your shadows will search for us," he answered smoothly, nodding toward DD at my shoulder.

"Brilliant." I beamed. "DD can do it. Gods aren't going to notice a shadow."

"Some will, Randy. Do not be mistaken, such a mission is not without its dangers."

I worried my lip and called DD toward my face so I could look it over. "If there's danger, you get a choice. You can stick with me if you want. Or you can slink around and do recon work. I won't be mad either way." I wanted DD to search, but I was also being honest. I didn't know what these gods were capable of and wasn't sure my little bit of DD knew either. It had helped often and been hurt often, and it had its own feelings and consciousness. It deserved choice so I'd give it, no matter what I wanted in the moment.

It stood still, unwavering, as if it stared into me, then made a slow dip down, then up—a sort of shadow ball nod if there ever was one.

"Thank you," I whispered to it, tears threatening at DD's willingness to do this for me. For Mia. It swooped close, rubbed my cheek, and I felt its worry, but also its courage and strength... its willingness to help. My heart did a flip in my chest, and I realized how much I loved the little black ball of shadow plastered to my side. "You be careful with yourself," I said in my big-sister voice, because it's what I'd say to Merry or Mia in similar circumstances.

It gave its sort of nod again then zipped toward Ny, who gave it explicit instructions. "Cover as much of the Palace as you can, but stick with hidden or less frequented areas. Speak with other shadows regarding what they've seen. If or when you find something, get back here and wait for us to return after the evening's events. If you find nothing, be sure to return by the time the night's entertainment ends."

DD shivered an assent, moved to the shadow surrounding us, and somehow communicated it wanted out. Ny's shadow obliged, opening a tiny hole for DD to squeeze through before it zoomed up to the ceiling. I watched it skim the swirling pattern there until I had to turn to see it shimmy its way through the tiniest crack above the large doors we entered. It was gone, which made me happy and sad.

Gareth's large tatted hand landed on my shoulder. "It will find Mia and come back here safe."

"You can't know that for sure," I said.

"I can hope, and with our brains, our power, and a little hope, I think we can make a hell of a lot happen."

I faced Gareth and Ny, so different yet so similar, at least in how I felt about them. How I needed them. How they both helped in everything. "I can't..." My voice croaked as I choked up about my feelings, the stupid things obviously not having any sense of timing and rearing up at a not-so-great time.

Ny was by my side in a flash, holding me in his arms. "Shush, sweetling. No need to speak on it now, good or bad. We must prepare to meet the gods, and we'll need all our wits about us there, to help us find the one responsible for all our troubles."

All our troubles, yes. Ny's missing book and power, Mia's kidnapping, the messy Starry Wisdom made of all those people for so many decades... Gareth's traumatic past and Harley's quest for justice. It all led here, to these gods in this sparkling place. Whatever hid in the shadows hid here. Luckily for us, I was made of shadows, so it wouldn't stay hidden for long. And those shadows in me roiled at the thought of being let loose in this place, being released to deal with the source of our troubles.

Eighteen

THE PROVISIONS NY HAD mentioned arrived with a knock and a flourish. A line of stony men and women carted in food, drinks, and three large trunks filled to bursting with clothes and jewels and other fancy things spilling out of their confines.

Ny lounged like a prince, Gareth sat stoic and straight on a settee, and I gawked. I couldn't help it. I also couldn't help my spark of interest when I saw a large gold tray of what looked like pastries being set down on a long buffet against the wall opposite the royal seating area space.

I moved to check out the mound of sweet-looking delights. It wasn't every day I could taste and examine godly baked goods. Ny's hand rose to wave me on in a go-ahead gesture, and I pulled myself back. I needed to remember to act far more deferential than I was used to acting.

"Thank you, Prince," I muttered. I even gave a bow, though I hoped none of the stone servants caught the smirk I hid behind the fall of my dark hair.

I weighed a small red lump in my hand, something that smelled like red bean paste and, oddly enough, time. Time as in the concept, not thyme the herb. How I knew it was time I couldn't say, but it sat right in my brain when I connected the unfamiliar scent with the word. I poked it with my forefinger, testing the texture and jiggle of the thing. It was fascinating to me, but the clicking of the doors brought my attention up sharp. The stone servants were gone.

Ny sauntered over with a smile and laid his wide, warm hand at the small of my back. "A good choice, sweetling."

"Is it safe for me to eat?" I asked, which made me feel like an idiot because I realized we hadn't eaten anything since we'd been in the Dreamlands, so I immediately blurted, "Why am I not hungry?"

"The Dreamlands are like our dreams, I suspect. Food isn't a requirement for our bodies here." Gareth looked toward Ny for confirmation, who smiled at him and nodded.

"It's been like over two days. Plus, I had to pee the one time and was kidnapped right after."

"Dreamlands are not the human realm. You are human and not human here, in a way. Time also functions differently, so a few days here is only a few hours where you are from. Your body is waffling between the needs of the two different realms. Add in your own magics and magical affinity here, you get an odd reaction to most physical needs."

Partially also explained the rise in my magic, the feeling like it wanted to get out and stretch its legs, run free, fight. Especially here, in Kadath. I nodded and pushed the questions of bodily functions and needs aside. Debates on physical and psychological needs in different realms were interesting, but we needed to motor.

"Please do try it, Randy. It is a sweet treat."

I shrugged and popped it in my mouth. The flavor was unlike anything I could describe because it literally was not of the human world. It was sweet umami with notes of outdoorsy things I couldn't name, and time. In my mouth, I felt the time roll there, get stuck and unstuck, dredge up memories in flashes so quick, they skipped across my brain without fully registering.

"Wicked," I whispered, touching my hand to my mouth and reveling in the sensation there. I was only dragged from my baker's drive to parcel out every single flavor in the thing by Gareth's grumbling scoff.

"Ostentatious, I know," Ny said, as I turned to see him pulling a crown from one of the trunks, "but, as with all such trappings, expected of me in Kadath."

"I take it our jeans-and-tee uniforms will need to be upgraded," I said, moving to a trunk with a silky slip of a what might have been a dress peeking out.

"Yes. We must change, and quickly. We're expected in the Great Hall a little late, but not late enough to cause offense."

The court politics Ny had traversed all his life were at play here. They were sticky and, for me and Gareth, wholly new and dangerous. I'd need to tread carefully, and it seemed I'd do so in a dress.

THE DRESS WASN'T BAD. I wasn't one to wear dresses all the time, like Merry, but I also wasn't totally against them. The one Ny had said would be fine for our initial meet with the gods was the top one I'd pulled out, a lilac silk calf-length sheath dress with a drape across the bust and waist. It managed to highlight my tits and hips while softening the curves of my tummy. I liked it, and the long looks from Gareth and Ny told me they liked it, so it'd be more than good for whatever gods we faced. I dug in the trunk until I came back up with a pair of thin, silver metal sandals to wear.

"These good to leave behind?" I asked Ny, holding up my boots and hoping he knew I was asking more about the silver key hidden inside than the boots themselves.

He nodded and said, "The trunks will keep everything secure."

I wanted to ask more, but we were low on time for twenty questions, so I shoved things aside and put the boots, and my silver key, at the very bottom of the big piece of luggage.

A line of stone guards escorted us back down to the marble entry and across the wide expanse into a large, round meeting room, lined with thrones. The magic hit me, a punch right to my gut, and my power reared up again all on its own, but I had kind of known what to expect and was able to grit my teeth and push through it. Gareth didn't waver, but his spine and jaw were tense, so he was feeling like me. Ny's power rolled out to meet theirs, and he kept up his lazy-hipped stroll without missing a beat.

The thrones weren't fully expected, but they gave me something to concentrate my mind on as we made our way across the room. Some looked similar in shape and construct, but each was different, specific to a time and place in human history—a time and place corresponding to the god hovering around it. A huge, old one-eyed dude stood beside a giant wooden throne carved with ravens and wolves. A beautiful woman with sun-kissed skin and long black curls stood next to a chair made of rainbows. Literal rainbows. I don't know how they'd made light solid enough for her to perch on, but there she was.

There were also not-so-human looking gods in attendance, some even I recognized from my smattering of knowledge of ancient world pantheons. Anubis, with his black jackal head and tightly muscled human chest on display, stood tall and cross-armed by a sturdy chair of cedar, copper, and gold.

Toward the apex of the circle, and several steps above the regular ring, sat an empty throne of pitch black, larger and higher than all the other thrones. It swooped and swirled, like night. Like shadows carved in onyx, which was also like the onyx crown perched on top of Ny's head. It was Ny's throne. We walked toward it while the others in the room managed to cast eyes down at Ny's steps but watch me and Gareth with varying degrees of interest. When Ny sat gingerly down in his seat, giving his sexy-as-hell, I-don't-care-about-anything lean, Gareth and I stood still by the arms. Ny plucked me up before I was settled and made me sit on his lap. He also pulled Gareth closer, moving him to half squat on the large right arm of his throne.

No one said anything for long, awkward seconds. Then a graying, big-bearded white man in a pristine white toga, the god closest to Ny's right side, stood from his seat and, in a literal boom, said, "Welcome to Kadath once again, Prince Nyarlathotep, the Crawling Chaos. All we have here is because of you. All we enjoy we enjoy at your leisure."

Each of the other gods, once again with varying interest, said, "Welcome," after his little speech.

Ny lolled his head to the side and said, "Zeus, I thank you for your warm welcome. I will not linger long in your halls, but I do have need at the moment."

"We will be happy to offer whatever you require, Your Grace," said a devastatingly beautiful brown woman draped in tropical flowers sitting a few thrones down on our left.

Ny nodded and continued. "I have need of the Library of Kadath."

"It is yours," Zeus said, his voice echoing in the large stone circular space. "Is there a particular question or issue you may wish to present to our ranks? We may be able to help in your endeavors."

Ny cut cold eyes to the man, and a beautiful woman at his side jumped in to say, "Of course, we do not wish to pry, Prince Nyarlathotep. Only offer our aid."

"Thank you, Hera, but I have brought my companions, Randy and Gareth, to aid me. They have many, many skills. All of which I appreciate." Ny purred the last, trailing a hand from the curve of my neck down my shoulder and arm. I shivered and my magic thrum sang for him. I knew everyone in the room noticed both, because they studied me now with more concern and curiosity.

"We are at your disposal, if you are in need," the huge old man I took to be Odin called in a gruff voice.

A nod from Ny, a pause, then a demand. "I will hear any concerns or issues at this time."

What followed was a really boring hour of gods complaining–about each other, about their servants, their quarters, the use or disuse of magic, their ability or inability to travel. I learned some stuff, sure. Gods could go to the human realm, they just needed permission by a council to do so, and when they were there, they didn't have a whole lot of magic. Apparently the Dreamlands preserved their power, but their magic had long ago diminished in the human world. Hence, why they had crossed over. They didn't have the juice or clout they were used to anymore. Now, all they could do is go hang out occasionally when they got bored or something.

I also learned the human gods were very human. They had good and bad human traits and characteristics, all of which shone in the time they had to complain to their official leader. Ny took it in stride and settled what issues he could, but he remained aloof. It was different than the way he'd interacted with the people in Dylath-Leen. He'd been warm and open there. Here, he was closed off and cold. It was likely a power dynamic thing, but I was out of my element. All I could do was listen, hopefully learn something, and try not to yawn when a young-looking Roman god was having a fit about something an Aztec god had said about the Roman Empire.

I fidgeted a little in my seat, and Ny shut down complaint time. Turning to Zeus, he gave a snide sniff and said, "I suppose there is entertainment this evening?"

"Of course, Your Grace. We will have a ball in your honor."

That was just as Ny had suspected, so yay for our good luck. "Very well," Ny said, patting my back and giving a gentle push so I'd rise. He stepped in front of

Gareth and me. "I'll go to the library and will not return until the ball."

No one replied to his statement. They immediately dropped into bows. He climbed down the steps and walked out of the Great Hall, his footfalls echoing in the silence as Gareth and I shuffled behind him.

Nineteen

THE LIBRARY WAS A bust. A gorgeous, lush, fabulous bust, but still a bust. We scoured as many books as we could in the three hours we had. It wasn't even a dent in the archives they had there. Gareth about creamed his librarian pants when he saw it, and he muttered about more time when we had to peel him away from all the books and ancient scrolls. Sadly, there wasn't time for cool books and parchment. We had a ball to attend.

I'd hoped DD would be back with info when we returned to Ny's chambers, but of course not. I rummaged through my trunk, pulling out fabrics and jewels and makeup a bit willy-nilly, if I was honest. I loved a good reason to get fancy, but espionage in a palace with a bunch of old gods from the human realm wasn't exactly my idea of a good time, so I was doing everything with more than a little annoyance.

"How'd all this get here, anyway? And why's everything so damn human?" I asked on a huff, holding new and ancient beauty products while I kicked a pair of black mules across the marble floor.

"The gods here hold on to their human connections. They tend to stay in their human forms, entertain themselves as humans do, wear human clothes. I do the same, lovely, and you've never had an issue."

"Because I like you," I said, more than a little grumpy.

He laughed, walking over to dig deep into the trunk, and pulled up a dress so black, it looked made of shadow, like my dream-walking robes. "This would suit, sweetling."

I shrugged and peeled out of my dress in the middle of the sitting room, standing there in only my underwear and shiny metal sandal things. Both Ny and Gareth froze and a zig of lust shot through me too, but I shut it down.

"No time." With a saucy smirk as I stepped into the dress without any undergarments, I said, "But glad I can still make you stupid."

Ny smacked his lips and Gareth muttered, "We're both definitely stupid for you."

I took a handful of stuff—a comb made from stone, a set of jeweled barrette things, a variety of makeup tubes and vials, and a necklace of carved black onyx similar to Ny's crown—and plopped down at a vanity in the corner of the bedroom. My magic swirled inside, a riot of shadow, as I started getting ready.

By the time I was done, my magic and I were both a little calmer. Only a little, but calmer. I stood back so I could see all of myself. It clung tightly to my breasts, belly, hips, and ass but puffed out in a mass of swirling black from mid-thigh down. The black shadows in at the bottom of the dress moved as if in a breeze, but there definitely wasn't one in the room. It swayed all on its own, which was disconcerting but also beautiful. The fabric was shot through with some type of glittering material which shone in a rainbow of dark colors when it caught the light—a riot of purples and grays and blues and greens giving the fabric a dark glow. It was form-fitting but comfortable and easy to move in, as if the thing literally moved along with my body.

The cut of the dress was simple but effective—long, strapless, and mermaid-style, with a sweetheart neckline showing my tits off nicely. With a bit of smoky eye, a red lip, and my black hair pulled back off my face to cascade down my back, I knew I looked good, even among gods.

"You look ravishing," Ny purred, walking up behind me with Gareth so I saw all three of us together. We made a gorgeous trio. Me, all softness and curves in black, and Ny in an all-black tuxedo, his usually floppy hair brushed off his face. However, Gareth's look was the true knockout for me, He was dressed like Mr. Freaking Darcy in a black waistcoat, vest, and tight pants, with a black silk cravat tucked into a stark-white shirt.

"Look at you, Right Honorable Sir Gareth Davis," I said as I gave him several up and downs.

"I never knew you had a regency weakness," he said, his voice low and gruff and full of promise.

I shrugged. "What red-blooded hetero girl who's read Austen and watched any adaptation doesn't?"

"Fair enough," he said and gave a soft bow, humor in his eyes.

"Yes, yes. We are all beautiful creatures, sure to turn the heads of the gods gathered in our honor. Which is the point," Ny replied.

Any humor or thoughts of regency fantasies fled. I sucked in a breath, steadied myself and my magic, and said, "Let's do this thing."

Gareth offered his arm as Ny exited the room first. We had secrets to uncover and, more importantly, a sister to find. Pronto.

"WHO KNEW BALLS GIVEN by the old gods of Earth would be so damn boring?" I said under my breath as, once again, Gareth walked with me around the perimeter of the ball room. The decor was astounding, magical lights flickering and floating. Flowers hung suspended in the air, opening and closing their blooms as intervals. Lush fabrics in satin and velvet lined every surface, and the gold-threaded marbled gleamed at our feet. And the gods themselves were boring, boring, boring.

Whenever Gareth and I talked to one alone, they yammered on about myths or ancient history and their once great reigns in a particular area of the world. Others asked inane questions about current technology. A good chunk simply ignored us. No one looked at us with disdain or sneers or anything. No way they'd be outright rude or openly hostile toward us in Ny's presence, though some sure looked like they wanted to.

A few were cordial. The woman with the rainbow throne complimented my dress and hair. Anubis spoke about the library with us, a conversation that really got Gareth going. Odin was gruff and short with his words. Zeus and Hera were smiling and gave us a few beats of small talk before moving on to who they considered more appropriate conversation partners.

Ny steered clear of us. We'd thought being divided might mean we'd have more opportunities to learn something useful. He was across the vast ballroom, talking to a lovely man and woman completely covered in gold body paint.

Gareth stopped us, and I dragged my eyes from Ny to see what had caused it. Gupan and Ugar stood in our path, wearing the same getup as earlier in the day and the same slight frowns in their eyes.

"Gareth and Randy," the talking one said, a slight incline of his head. "We do hope you are enjoying your stay in Kadath."

"It's lovely," I answered, which was true. It was gorgeous, though also boring and likely the place where my sister was being held captive, and therefore a shitty place.

"You should be honored. There have been no humans in Kadath in centuries," the one who talked said.

"In centuries? Really? Everyone seems so happy to speak with us, it would seem like they are used to humans." I hoped to draw out more, see if they knew anything about Mia, because this was the closest I'd come to having any type of relevant convo with the gods.

"I wasn't speaking of you. You are... not exactly human," he said, turning back to Gareth.

"What's that supposed to mean?"

"You are more than. He is clearly a wielder of magic. You are... more."

"How do you know?"

The one who never spoke opened his mouth and said, "Because our magic wants to meet yours."

"Meet hers how?" Gareth asked, pulling me tighter to his side.

The talking one smirked, then he said, "We wish her no harm. We only wish to know why you are here, now."

"We are all at the service of Prince Nyarlathotep," Gareth answered.

"True. However, I believe some of us may be more in his service than others. Some may chaff there." As the talking one said this, the silent one turned his head to stare across the room at a grouping of gods. Zeus, Hera, Odin, and a fourth I had yet to meet huddled together, staring hard at Ny from their positions.

"He sees and knows," said the quiet one, nodding toward Ny, who'd swung his head at the group before they scattered.

"Has he always known those four don't like him?" I asked.

"In so much as gods don't like bowing to others, yes. In their more recent activities, I would say not." His lips were a hard line, pressed so firmly together, they lost their color. Without another word, they stepped aside and Gareth tugged my arm until my feet started moving once again.

"Quick and maybe a little too easy and obvious," I muttered.

"Possibly," Gareth said, his head cocked in thought. "I'd like to get closer."

"Go ahead," I said, dropping his arm. "We should split up again anyway. Someone else might talk to one of us alone more easily."

"I won't leave you alone here." Gareth stood firm, so I gave him a soft shove.

"Go on now. Get." We both chuckled and I said, "Do you really think anyone here would do something to me with Ny right in front of us?"

The stiffness left Gareth's posture and he shook his head.

"Then go," I said. "Try to find out more. Maybe flirt with some goddess for answers."

His calm was diminished, betraying his worry, but he did what I asked, stepping away to move closer to the still-huddled group of four gods.

I stood unsure for a moment, until a stone servant passed with wine. After snatching a glass, I eased over to the food tables, happy to see so many desserts again but far more focused on staying silent and fading slightly into the shadows of the wall to covertly listen as others passed by for food and drinks.

I hid there, still and shrouded by my magic, until I felt a presence shift in beside me. I hadn't seen anyone coming or noticed anyone even seeing me there, so it was a shock. I looked at a very tall but otherwise non-descript guy beside me. Average face, average skin, average brown hair. All of it defied any type of meaningful thought or description. Power didn't radiate off him, which was odd. Everyone here had power. He didn't feel godlike, but I knew he couldn't be a human, so I was confused as hell.

He grinned, his mouth a little lopsided, and rocked back on his plain black men's loafers with his hands casually stuck in his pockets. "Having a good time?" he asked.

"Sure." I shrugged. "You?"

He shrugged back, grinning. "Better now that I get to speak with you."

I huffed and waved a dismissive hand at him, then turned it to offer my palm. "My name's Randy. I don't remember seeing you earlier. You are?"

"Not supposed to be here," he said with a tight laugh as he took my hand. He brought it up to his lips and pressed a soft, wet kiss to the back. The contact crackled with magic I couldn't gauge or place, but it made my heartbeat faster and my own magic shiver in fear in my chest.

"Come. Dance with me."

It was a happy command but clearly a command, and I couldn't stop myself from obeying. He stepped out of the shadow with me, and more power than I'd ever felt melted out of his being, unfurling, and crashed over me in electric waves, nearly making my back bow and knees buckle. I froze, my muscles and magic screaming at the feeling, but he pulled me along effortlessly, commanding my body in some way. Gasps went up around the room a second before the gods and stone servants all dropped to their knees, bowing with foreheads pressed firmly to the marble floor. I could taste their fear and awe in the air toward whoever this dude was.

Ny moved toward us, head down in a deference I'd never seen, but the man waved a hand, freezing him in place like Wilbur had done back in Columbus. Gareth also looked frozen in mid-stride. I tried to get my hand out of the man's grip, but it was firm and strong as he pulled me to the center of the floor, placed me in his arms, and began a slow waltz to a flute tune he conjured out of thin air.

I had no choice but to follow. I said nothing because I was terrified and certain this was the guy, the one who had Mia. I frantically looked at him again and tried to step out of the dance, but found myself unable. I was dancing with this guy whether I liked it or not.

"It's not very nice to force a woman to dance," I said.

He laughed. "I suppose it's not. I simply wanted to speak with you without anyone interrupting us."

"We could've talked in the shadows."

"True, but then these creatures wouldn't have also seen it."

"Not a fan of the gods?"

He surveyed the room as if he was giving the question serious thought, like he wanted to be utterly honest and sure in whatever he gave. It wasn't hesitancy to speak out of fear. He didn't fear anyone in the room, and for good reason given his power. "Some more than others. They all have their issues, which is why I normally steer clear."

"You came tonight."

"Only to see you, Miranda Carter," he said, his voice deep and old and something twining through me in a rush of magic.

"Randy," I said on a gasp, out on reflex.

"Apologies." He let out a sharp, hard laugh. "Randy it is. A true pleasure to see you once again and meet you, different yet oh-so similar as you are, were, and will remain."

"We've met before?"

"You could say we have and have not. Not you, but another who was and is and will be."

Cryptic nonsense. "Again, what's your name?"

He gave me the lopsided grin and a twirl out before pulling me close. "King Azathoth."

I froze like Ny, like Gareth, but not actually, because Ny's sire kept me dancing.

"I haven't been to Kadath in millennia, but I saw you coming now and then and before and knew in the future I'd want this, so here I am. For one dance."

I didn't know what to say, couldn't really say anything, so I let him pull me along in the dance, humming in my ear the whole time, until the music faded slowly. He freed me and bowed deep.

"Randy Carter. A true honor and pleasure. I've known you before and hope to know you again." He leaned forward and planted a kiss in the middle of my forehead. It wasn't sexual, more fatherly and super weird. It made my magic flare and churn in my gut again, screaming to get out. "A kiss, for your key," he whispered. In a blink, he was gone, and Ny was at my side, grabbing my hand.

"Come. Now," he growled at Gareth, unconcerned with niceness or how any of it looked. No one saw the scene though, because they were all still too terrified, shaking heads plastered to the marble floor and not daring to look up as the flavor of Azathoth's power lingered in the air all around us.

Twenty

NY WASTED NO TIME dragging us up to his quarters. He literally hissed at a contingent of stone men attempting to follow us, and they dropped back real quick. We slammed through the doors, and Ny immediately covered us in shadows. He spun me into his arms and hugged me tightly to his chest, his head landing on mine. His breathing was deep, ragged, unsteady and his arms shook around me. I realized he was terrified, and it made my own fear over the encounter with his father-sire rise even more. My magic was quivering, shaking, but not hiding, so I was able to take in the gentle taps telling me DD was attempting to get through.

"DD wants in," I muttered to Ny, who didn't outwardly do anything but must have dropped a part of his defenses because DD came zipping into the shadows circling the three of us. It skidded to a halt, hovering a few feet away, and I felt its uncertainty at the situation.

Gareth also felt uncertain. I was buried against Ny's chest so I couldn't see where he was, but I heard his voice move closer and felt a firm press on Ny from behind as Gareth asked, "Ny? Are you okay? You have a handle on yourself?"

"What even was that?" I asked, the muffled question possibly lost in Ny's chest, right against his frantically beating heart.

Ny's breath, still slightly broken, shuddered in and out a few times before he straightened his body and pushed me out to arm's length, sweeping over me with his eyes. "Oh, sweetling, are you well? Did he harm you?"

So many questions lingered from all of us, with no answers, so I calmed myself and tried to get control. "I'm fine. We danced. No big." My voice cracked in the middle of my attempted nonchalance.

Ny smoothed his hands over my hair, down my shoulders, and took my hands in his, then he studied them, the hands his father had held only moments before. He closed his eyes, visibly shook himself, and opened them again to reveal his starry nebulous gaze, the one he threw out when magic rode hard through him. "My sire's appearance was unexpected."

"No shit," I said, moving to flop down on one of the settees. "It was intense, for sure."

"I didn't realize Azathoth traveled outside the darker recesses of the cosmos," Gareth said. It wasn't framed as a question, but he clearly wanted answers from Ny, who came to sit close to me on the settee. Our thighs touched, his hand went to my knee, and he squeezed, as if reassuring himself I was still there.

"Word of his blindness and idiocy is greatly exaggerated," he muttered. "He does not leave the cosmos often, and rarely travels into other realms, but he is what made me, and therefore he holds all the power I possess and more. He can travel wherever he wishes, whenever he wishes. He simply wishes not to do so very often."

"What about your siblings?" Gareth asked.

"They are truly trapped in the cosmos unless they are invited in by someone. King Azathoth shared his interdimensional powers with me so I could serve as a messenger and emissary of sorts for his court."

I was trying to straighten the connections in my head. "The cosmic court, which is different from the Dreamlands court, which is different from this court made up of the Other Gods residing here in exile."

"Yes. Imagine each court, each ruler, as a little castle. I'm in charge of many castles, but my sire is the ruler over me and all under me, and all other who have any power in this realm or any other, whether they realize it or not."

"Okay." I didn't get it, not really. Maybe I couldn't get it because it was too much infinity and power and omnipresence for a regular person from the human realm to really understand. What I did understand was the blast of power he allowed me to feel. He allowed me to feel it, because I know he hid it for a few minutes while we talked in the shadows. Why he did either, and why he wanted to dance with me and talk in weird time-loop riddles, was beyond what I wanted to understand at the moment. Still, Ny made me tell him word for word what his father had said.

"Your father knows Randy is important. Why she's important to him specifically is unknown," Gareth said.

Ny closed his eyes and dropped his head back, deep in thought. Shaking himself out of it, he looked between me and Gareth, "There's been a number of interesting developments regarding Randy's power and possible position since we've been in the Dreamlands."

"The Oracle talked about my power and gave me a silver key and the ghouls bowed to me for whatever reason."

"Don't forget what the twins told us before King Azathoth showed up," Gareth said.

"What is this?"

I waved it off. "They just said they felt my magic."

"Not only felt it, was somehow called by it."

Ny studied my face. "Has your magic been acting different in the Dreamlands?"

I worried my lip, trying to think of everything I could or should say about it. The magic stuff was so hard to describe, but I knew a few points were important. "I felt DD's tether or connection or whatever more solidly. I felt the shadow we rode, and somehow I just knew I could command it if I tried. Here in Kadath, my magic has been antsy. Like it wants to come out. Or, maybe more like lash out."

"We've yet to encounter any of the Writhing, even here where it likes to lurk among the power of the gods, but I suspect you could also connect with it more easily in this plane, given all you've said and what you've done in the past," Gareth said for me, though it was speculation.

"I think the Dreamlands might be able to offer you more answers regarding your power—the thing you always wished to know about where your power comes from and what it means."

I hadn't thought of it because my focus was Mia and survival in the few days I'd been here, but he was right. My magic felt different here, easier in some ways, so I'd probably be able to explore it more fully. Maybe find out more about it and, by extension, myself. None of it mattered when we'd come to the Dreamlands for one thing and one thing only: Mia.

"Doesn't matter. I can find out more another time. What matters now is getting Mia out of here." I didn't want to ask the next question, but it needed to be asked. "Do you think your sire took her? He froze you like Wilbur did."

"No," Ny said. "Wilbur reworked my own magic against me, using a spell to do so. He didn't force magic on me as my sire did tonight. Whoever helped Wilbur, controls Wilbur, needs my power for some reason and must resort to trickery to take or mitigate it. King Azathoth has no reason to steal my power. He has more than enough of his own."

"We put aside the scary king business for now and focus on the original goals of getting Mia and your powers back." I looked to the still-hesitant DD and asked, "What'd you find?"

It swooped down, caressing Ny's ear as if whispering there.

"A human woman and a ghoul are being held in one of the north tower rooms," Ny said, jumping up as he spoke.

"Gotta be her. Let's get there. Now."

"Wait," Gareth said, putting a hand on my chest to stop my steps. "We don't know what's guarding her or who holds her."

"Doesn't matter. We go in guns blazing, or magic blazing, I guess. You didn't bring a gun with you, right, Gareth?"

Gareth shook his head as Ny talked over him. "It would be best we slow for a moment and discuss," Ny said, backing up Gareth with words and with his presence close to the mage's back.

"Seems obvious to me. It's one of the four gods with their little secret huddle in the ball."

"You refer to Zeus, Hera, Odin, and Discordia?"

I snorted. "Of course a god named Discordia would be involved."

"They all chafe at their place in this court, as rulers who must in turn be ruled. However, they've never attempted to cross me before."

"Does it necessarily mean they wouldn't cross you now?" Gareth asked.

"No."

"The twins pointed them out to us, so I think they think they're shady as hell. Did you find anyone else who might be a suspect?"

Ny shook his head now. "All have the same petty grievances, as far as I know. Yet their obvious actions in the ballroom... It all appears too pointed to make me believe they are the culprits."

"It's the stupidity of power." When Gareth and Ny looked at me all blank-faced, I explained. "You know, like when people have so much power they assume they're above the law or something and do whatever they want all willy-nilly out in the open?"

"They can't possibly be so stupid," Gareth scoffed.

"Sure they can. Anyone with power can be. Power makes some people rise to the occasion, be and do better. It also makes some people stupid assholes."

Ny had his creased-brow thinking face on and I watched, fascinated, as it slowly morphed into something cold and dangerous. "If it is any of the four, or even all four, they will pay for their actions."

"Good. All settled. It's one of those four or all four of them, and we're off to kick ass and take names."

Gareth sighed but stripped off his tight jacket and vest, leaving his billowy white shirt and cravat in place. Ny stayed in his tux. I twisted my long hair and used the jeweled barrettes to clip it out of the way as best I could. The metal sandals were cute but had already left blisters, so I hurried to the trunk to retrieve my boots. I didn't want to take the time to shimmy out of my dress, so a magic fight in fancy attire it was.

Finally all situated, I looked at my guys and asked, "We go in swinging?"

"In so many words. DD leads. I will handle any gods in the room. Gareth, you take on any other creatures if they are in attendance. Randy, your sole focus is Mia. Get her free and out of the tower by any means necessary." Ny fished out the pocket watch and handed it to Gareth. "You may need this."

I sent thanks to DD and urged it along as I also asked it to bring my spear forward. It popped into my hand quickly, heavier than ever before. A solid, glistening weapon with a pulse matching the thrum in my gut. Another weird magical point, but no time to dwell. We had godly ass to kick and a baby sister to save.

THE GODS WERE BORING and stupid and cliché, it seemed. The tower where Mia was being held was high, isolated, and accessed only through a narrow, winding staircase. It was something right out of a fairytale, except the princess we were after had a pixie cut and couldn't let us climb up her hair. Hair climbing would be kind of gross anyway.

DD led us right up to a door. We'd had no problems getting there, so we burst into the room at the top of a spiraling northern tower.

All I saw was Mia, slumped against a wall. Her jeans and tee were dirty and torn, and Ny's vest was equally messed up but still secure on her. Her head hung down and her hands were lifted in the air and connected to old-timey looking manacles. She didn't move when we entered, and we weren't subtle about entering.

I didn't think. I reacted. Running forward, I slammed to my knees, only stopping to cut a death glare toward the dude chained beside Mia who'd started growling at me for some reason.

"Back off," I said, and my magic pulsed out of my body, casting shadows all around.

The guy started, then diverted his eyes. He let out a small whine as he bowed his head at me and said, in an altogether not-human voice, "You're the sister."

"Oh, Miranda Carter is more than a mere sister." I knew the voice and bolted up to stand between it and my sister, the thing who'd taken her away in the first place.

Gareth and Ny faced off with Wilbur against one wall of the room, but he didn't look alarmed. Not at all.

A crackle of thunder and flash of lightening, and there was Zeus, leering at us from the wall opposite Wilbur. "Good to see everyone now in attendance," he said, his uppity tone of voice grating my nerves.

Yep, we'd been right, and he'd been cliché and stupid. I waited a beat, to see if anyone else jumped in, before asking, "All by yourself?"

He brushed imaginary dirt from his white robes and answered, "While a handful of others share my desires and will help when the time comes, they did not need to be concerned with the particulars."

"The desire to be a jackass?" I asked.

Lightening flashed toward me, searing up my legs in a hot flash of pain before Ny could wrangle it back and away. "Your insolence is not appreciated, Miranda."

"It's Randy." I seethed, using anger to push through the lingering pain in my lower half.

He waved a hand. "It is no matter. Soon, all of you will be neutralized, I will have accessible powers in the human realm, and those loyal to me will be given back their rightful places amongst the humans. All thanks to the books." Suddenly, an old, heavy-looking locked book appeared in his hands.

Ny jerked, as if having to stop himself from racing toward it. Clearly it was the Book of Knowing, and Mia, still not responsive, was the other book.

"Books you can't fully read," the guy next to Mia called as he made eyes at Ny, trying to communicate something. His bow and those eyes told me he must be the ghoul friend, Richard Pickman, but it didn't matter. Nothing mattered but freeing Mia, getting Ny his book, and kicking some godly ass while we were at it.

"All I need is time, which is something I will soon have in abundance," he said as he tapped the locked cover of the Book of Knowing. "I've also managed to extract a number of interesting spells from the Necronomicon, even if the entirety of the text remains locked in the human's mind. I'll break her and retrieve the completed text soon enough."

It was my turn to growl. "Like hell you will."

"Oh, Miranda. You think you have power here, in my palace?"

"My palace," Ny hissed. "My land. My rule. You forget yourself, Zeus, and I plan to make you remember."

A wicked smile flashed across the god's face and a rumble of thunder sounded. "I do believe, without all your power, we are more evenly matched than you suspect, Ny." The abbreviated name was a sign of disrespect and a taunt. Ny and Richard Pickman growled, shadows began to swirl everywhere, and Gareth's death stare locked on the now-silent Wilbur as his sigils flared to life.

It was time to fight, and we all had a lot to fight for, so without another word, I whirled and struck Mia's chains with my spear, sending shadows and sparks flying in my wake.

Twenty One

MIA'S HEAD SNAPPED UP as soon as my spear struck her chains. "Randy?" she asked with disbelief shading her voice. As if I wouldn't have moved heaven and earth to get to her.

"I got you, sis," I said through clenched teeth. "Just close your eyes a sec." When she did as I asked, I banged the chains with more force, sending more magic flying every which way. I heard the fight going on behind me, felt the snap and crackle of magic in the air, but I had a singular focus. Get Mia out of there. I trusted Ny and Gareth to take care of the rest. I had to trust them to take care of the rest.

DD bounced in my vision, trying to get my attention. When I stopped, it zipped up to the ceiling, and for the first time since coming into the Dreamlands, I saw the Writhing in the shadowy flesh. DD wanted me to use it, and who was I to argue about it when so much was at stake?

I called it down and it followed my lead, creeping over the rough, dark stone wall until it reached my sister's hands. "Free her," I said, and it obeyed without question, its dark power pulsing over the chains, wiggling into the lock, and snapping the manacles open with surprising speed. Mia slumped over, the upper half of her body collapsing after being held upright in an arm-raised position for who knew how long. She breathed, slow and deep, before she croaked out, "Rich."

I looked over at the ghoul and saw his eyes, pointed on my sister, were full of concern. I told the Writhing to free him as well, and it wasted no time. His arms fell, but he did not. He scooted over toward me, more toward Mia, actually, as he rubbed his arms. "Mia? Mia?" he called, his voice aching.

"All good over here," she muttered into my arms as I rocked her slowly.

"I'm getting you out of here. Now."

Mia rose, then looked behind me, her eyes wide. "No," she said with such horror, I couldn't help but turn.

Wilbur had Gareth by his throat, wringing the life from him. Ny was fighting Zeus, but the speed and flashes of lightening and shadow were too much for me to track clearly with my eyes, so I couldn't tell if either had the upper hand in the moment. Gareth certainly didn't.

"Help him," my sister said.

Rich scooped her slumped body into his arms, cradling her tight. "Go. They need you now. I have Mia."

I bit my lip. He looked capable enough, and Mia wanted him there for whatever reason. Ny trusted him. I had to take a leap too. I kissed my sister on the forehead. "Be right back, Mia," I said and whirled around to face Wilbur.

Without letting go of the Writhing, I redirected it. "Hold him." It obeyed, moving quickly to reach Wilbur, who dropped Gareth as soon as he felt the shadows clinging to his boots. I scrambled over to my big guy, who was coughing on the floor. "You good?"

He cleared his throat and shook his head. "Yes," he said on a rasp. "Thank you."

"No problem. Can you fight?"

He flexed his hands, his sigils flaring to life. "Yes." He stood as he slid a hand in his pocket and brought out the pocket watch, then drained it of all the power in one go. He glowed black faintly, and I could swear I saw stars and space circling.

"Make that fucker pay," I said, and he nodded, flexing his arms.

Wilbur had managed to shake off the Writhing somehow and faced us again. "All mere parlor tricks, Miranda. You nor Gareth have the power to sustain an attack."

"Don't need to sustain shit if we kill you quick," I said but made no move. I hated this dude, but Gareth hated him more, and had for longer. I stepped aside to let Gareth do his thing.

He didn't disappoint. His sigils flared and his hand flickered with the odd grayish glow. It was Crumbling Flame, the same spell he'd used to take down the black church. He flung the flame straight at Wilbur's torso, which exploded in a mass of fire. The spell tried to burrow into him, crawling across his body and toward his mouth to get in and tear him down from the inside out.

Wilbur's body shook, but he didn't panic. His power flared with the sickly yellow light he'd used on me, and Gareth's flame sputtered out, leaving only a decayed black mark on Wilbur's chest. Looked like it hurt like hell, which was good, but it wasn't slowing the dude down any.

With a flick of his wrist, he slammed me with the yellow light again, but I'd seen it coming this time. I threw up a barrier of the Writhing between us, and his light was swallowed up whole by the dark I controlled. Wilbur tried another spell, which also slid off the tentacle shadows without any problems. The Writhing was a strong barrier. However, he was keeping us on the defensive, and we didn't have a whole lot of time in this attack. The more power Gareth used, the more he was drained. I also didn't know how long I'd be able to keep up. My magic had failed against Wilbur before, with dire consequences. It also kept us from doing anything to him.

"Randy," Gareth said. He took my hand and kissed it quickly. "Let me do this."

I nodded, stepping back with my barrier of Writhing to let Gareth step forward. He wanted to take out the bad guy who'd haunted his nightmares for a decade, and I wouldn't stop him.

"Holler if you need anything," I called, and Gareth gave a feral grin. He'd charged, regrouped, and was ready to tear down Wilbur piece by piece. I'd laugh if there wasn't another fight to the death happening behind me, and my sister wasn't huddled in the arms of a ghoul on the floor of this janky tower room.

"We need to leave. Now." I attempted to grab Mia from Rich's arms, but he shook his head.

"Ny," he whispered, and I looked toward where the two gods stood still, Ny writhing in blue-white power and hovering a few inches off the floor. A flash of light blinded me, and the smell of ozone tinged the air. Suddenly, Ny was standing and Zeus was crumpled on the floor, unmoving.

"Ny!" I rushed over. "Are you okay? Is he dead?"

"Wait!" Mia screamed, trying to catch me, stop me, but I was too hopped up on worry and adrenaline and she was too weak.

I hugged my Prince to me, trying to feel with my body he was whole and good, but my body told me something else. My magic didn't thrum in my gut for Ny as it always had. It screamed a warning, harsh and jarring. I jerked up to look at Ny's face, now set in a beatific smile I'd never seen before.

"Dear Miranda, you are a lovely creature. Maybe I'll keep you after all."

Ice water splashed over my spine. This wasn't Ny. Son of a bitch, this was not my Ny.

I tried to jump back, but I was in his arms, and he branded me tight. He leaned down, taking a deep breath, a deep smell from my hair. "Yes. You would be delicious. I can sense it, the way this body craves you. Ny's screaming in here, raging for me to release you. Why would I when I can have so much fun with you both now?"

Lightning flashed in his eyes, and I knew somehow Zeus was in there. Hadn't known such a thing was possible but it was certain. Zeus had somehow taken over Ny's human body and pushed the Outer God aside in there, trapping him.

Mia yelled, "Transference! It's body transference, a spell from the Necronomicon."

Shit. Not good at all. I didn't know how to, or even if I could, undo a Necronomicon spell. Once again, I cursed my lack of magic knowledge, my newbie status.

"Let go of me," I yelled, struggling. I'd dropped my spear by Mia, so I couldn't use it. DD was already bouncing around, trying to wiggle between us and free me somehow without success. Zeus-as-Ny was somehow able to repel DD, much like regular Ny was able to communicate and call to DD. Zeus seemed to have access to the Prince's powers when in his body.

I didn't know what to do; too much was happening and I couldn't think clearly. All I knew was I didn't have enough knowledge or power to do much. I looked at the floor and saw the Writhing was there, waiting, and I had a flash of realization. My dreams, the Oracle's words. I knew what I needed to do, even if it meant bad things down the line. I knew I needed to become something else if I was going to have any chance of helping here, and my access to something else was lodged firmly in my combat boot.

"Take me," I said.

Zeus smiled, I assumed because the ass thought I was talking to him. I wasn't. I was commanding the Writhing, and it knew the difference. I felt it creep up my feet and over my calves, swallowing me piece by piece in its churning, ancient power. Zeus, the idiot, didn't catch on until I'd been half taken, all shadow from the belly button down.

"No," he commanded, holding me tighter. It was futile on his part. He didn't know, but I knew. The Writhing knew. Ny had always known. I was made of shadow, and I could return to it whenever I wanted.

As it twisted around me, pushing his arms away to take me piece by piece, I stared hate into Zeus's eyes. It climbed up my neck, and before it reached my mouth and swallowed me whole, I said, "See you soon, asshole." Then, I was all darkness.

I BLINKED MY EYES open and saw I was in the cave of my dreams. Like I'd figured. I was at the well, with the Writhing pouring off my body and filling up the indentation. Now I had to figure out what to do next, how to become something or someone who could take out a god who'd somehow taken over an Outer God. No small feat, any of it.

Fidgeting, I smoothed my hands down my dirty gown. The fabric still moved, still held together without any tears or holes, which was a minor miracle itself. "Okay, Randy," I whispered out loud to myself, "time to get your shit together."

A throat cleared to my left, and I froze. No one'd ever been in my cave dream, so I was more than a little unsure about how to proceed.

A dark voice, low and high, soft and firm... duality and opposition given sound, said, "Who has come to the gate?"

I slowly turned and found a huge figure in dark robes, something like every rendition of the grim reaper I'd ever seen, except I couldn't see their skull face. I was sure they were a they and had a skull face though.

"I'm Randy Carter," I said, straightening my spine. If I was going to fight this thing too, I'd do it not cowering. I was sick to death of cowering. No more.

"Ah. Miranda 'Randy' Carter, of Columbus Ohio, United States, human realm."

I nodded, more than a little curious how they knew where I lived, but I didn't ask questions. I stared, waiting for them to continue.

"Come, come. There is little time, and you have a choice to make."

They threw a globe of light in the air, illuminating us and the huge gate I finally noticed behind them. It reached higher than I could see and looked like tarnished silver, the dingy browns and greens streaked through with glimpses of the shining metal. The bars of the gate were intricate curlicues marked with symbols. All of it looked very much like the key I had tucked in my combat boots, snuggly lodged between my foot and the boot insole.

"I, uh, don't have a lot of time."

"Time is relative, as you are well aware, Ms. Carter."

"Fair enough. Who are you though?"

The robed figure gave a slight bow of their head. "I am Umar at-Tawil."

Yep. Seemed about right. This was the gate my key unlocked. The gate to the outer cosmos. The robed figure was Ny's brother's guard guy. Knowing it didn't help me a whole lot. None of it seemed cool for me.

"I didn't realize I'd been dreaming of the gate," I said.

"You've dreamed of this place? Interesting. I had not realized. I only knew to expect you one day, as per my master's instructions."

"What else did he say about me?"

"He said you'd smell of moonlight, shadow, and the king."

The last bit startled me. The king, who I'd danced with. The one who'd held me for a waltz, then kissed my forehead. Seems he'd left some type of scent on me.

They went on, not skipping a beat, "Your choice, Randy, is simple. You may enter the gate with your key and, by entering, come to learn the power of the cosmos. You may use the key on yourself, to unlock the last of your power, the parts you were not ready to know or use. Or, you may return to the human realm, without any magic or the concerns that come along with it."

"So ultimate power, my own extra power, or no power at all?"

"Exactly, it is a difficult—"

"My power, please," I said, cutting them off.

They cocked a head at me. "So quick to choose. Are you certain?"

"I don't need all the cosmic power business. I think what I have inside will help us enough, with Gareth and Ny at my back. And I do need to get back, like real quick, so if we could speed up the process or whatever, that'd be great."

"You're giving away cosmic power, power on par with the full strength of Prince Nyarlathotep."

"I get it. I do, and I don't want it. Never did. I just wanted to run a bakery and have a good life with people

I love. Can't exactly be a regular-smegular person anymore, if I ever was, but I can get as close as possible. As close as possible doesn't include ultimate cosmic power in some far-off realm of space and time. It also requires I have some power, the power to save the people I love. I can't pretend I can give it all up and go back to whatever I thought was 'normal.' Though, to be honest, I was never 'normal,' so whatever. I need power, but not ultimate power. Just enough of a boost to get us out of our current shit storm, please and thank you."

"You choose to stifle your potential for power and yet still keep the responsibility of power?"

"Yep. Sure do. To get back to the people I love and be able to help them. It's really no choice at all." It wasn't. Oddly, my mind was perfectly clear when presented with the choice. My angst about my power was point-less because I was my power, like I was shadow. Like Ny had always said, had hoped I would see. And I was seeing clearly there and then. I wasn't power hungry like Zeus or willing to give up power at the expense of people I loved. I was, finally, content to be who I was, no more and no less, for myself and for them.

A soft chuckle. "I am surprised and pleased with you, Ms. Carter."

"Yeah, okay. Thanks, I guess, but seriously, can we get on with this? My sister and my guys need me back in the Dreamlands."

"Very well. Hand me your key."

I knelt to undo my boots and shook the key into my palm. Its silver glowed in a pulse, like a heartbeat. Its heartbeat sped up as I turned it over to the guard. "Here you are."

They held it up between bone fingers and studied the thing. "All seems to be in order. Now, this may hurt." Pain seared through my chest as their hand shot out, thrusting the key through my flesh, past my ribs, and straight into my heart.

Twenty Two

I'D THOUGHT THE SHADOW walking hurt. It had, but not nearly like this. I'd been unmade in the shadows and reformed, except the sensation had been purely physical. The pain from the key seared through my blood like acid, a physical, burning sensation. However, underneath the physical reaction was something else, something other. Something rending what made me, pulling me apart and stitching it back together. My soul, aura, whatever it was called, was being torn to shreds, then glued into a new pattern. The process the key unlocked in me unraveled me physically, psychically, and magically. I held on to who I was and what I knew, but it felt like a near call, as if at any second, everything I was and had been could blow away, leaving room for a new thing taking up space in my body and mind.

I gritted my teeth—metaphorically of course because all this was somehow metaphysical as hell—and held on tight, riding out the pain of disassembly and rearrangement by holding on to what I wanted to keep tight: all my loves and desires and certainties about who and what I was, even if those things sometimes wavered when I overthought before. In the place I was, fear and agony and newness crowded in and threatened to unmake me in every way, not allow me to come back together in a stronger form. I clung to what I knew and did not question. I didn't doubt. My new certainty allowed me to push through and become something newly me, not just wholly new.

I couldn't explain how all of it happened, what the magic was or the theory behind it. Harley or Ny would know, be able to explain the process away in some smart occult language I didn't have because I didn't know enough about the theory or practice of magic in the abstract. However, the lack of knowing particulars no longer mattered, because just as I was shadow, I knew then I was also magic.

My magic had been a piece of me before, locked in my gut. A thrum plucked occasionally, rising up when called forward, intentionally or unintentionally. The acid of my blood mellowed to a song with a heavy bass beat. My magic wasn't an isolated thrum any longer. It was me. It sustained me now. It beat with my life, and the beat was strong. A level of power as strong as I felt among the gods of Earth. Not as strong as King Azathoth, but as strong as Ny's without his Book of Knowing.

I felt myself stuffed back into my body, a body which was still quasi-human, still me in shape and form but also not. It was something more, as so many had said to me already. I wasn't fully human. I was shadow, time, and magic released and realized. I could taste it on my tongue, the same way I knew time was an ingredient in the odd sweet in Ny's chamber or could tell the difference in the atmosphere of the Dreamlands itself, the same way I knew what sugar variants went into a cookie I tried for the first time at home. The natural talent of a strong palate, only my palate now knew magic, not just baking ingredients.

I opened my eyes and looked around me. Nothing seemed to have changed. The cave's slick black stone walls were there, Umar at-Tawil stood stock-still looking exactly the same. The Writhing did its writhing thing in the well, which I knew for certain was the cosmic source of the Writhing itself, the place from which it had come to be, just as it was now the place the new me had come into being.

I looked down at myself and I saw shadows. Not DD, which wasn't anywhere around. Something I would worry about if it hadn't been the same in my dreams. DD was back where I had come from, and I'd be back too. Soon. This shadow was me, my magic... a dark wave flowing out of me and into the world connected to nothing other than my essence. It was different than the DD attracted to me because it was internally constructed and pushed out, pieces of my magic making itself known to the outside world.

"This going to be around me all the time, like Pigpen's cloud of dirt?" I grumbled, waving my hand in front of my face to watch the smudge of shadow trail a half second behind.

"You are your magic, Ms. Carter," the guard replied, though to be honest my question was more to myself than them.

I hummed, feeling a beat in my blood, the beat of magic now giving me life and power—so much power that if I focused on it too long, it made me dizzy and giddy. I didn't have the luxury to experiment now, however. I needed to get back to the tower.

"Are we done here?" I didn't mean to come off as flippant or harsh, but I had places to be, people to save."

"Almost," Umar at-Tawil said. They held out their bony hand, palm up, and presented me with the silver key once again.

"I'm good," I said at the offer. I'd made my choice. I didn't need to be back here, ever again.

"You are good, Ms. Carter. You are also the holder of the key. I cannot take it from you."

"You didn't take it. I gave it to you."

They shook their head. "Mere semantics. It is yours and so must stay in your possession, until such time as it can be released."

"When's that going to be?"

"When you no longer have use for it."

I grabbed the thing to stop the back and forth. I didn't want it, didn't think I'd ever need it, but objects of power or whatever seemed to have their own mind.

If Umar at-Tawil said I had to keep it, I'd keep it. Didn't mean I'd need to use it. Maybe I'd just know when to pass it on to someone else, like the Oracle had done with me.

"It's been nice meeting you?" It came out like a question because I wouldn't really call it nice, more like confusing, then super painful, then enlightening in weird ways. My Midwestern manners had forced me to say the nice thing.

Umar at-Tawil gave a small bow and a sweep of their arm.

I stood there, waiting a few seconds, then turned around in a circle. "Um, how exactly do I get back?"

"All you need you now have," they said.

Okay. Great. No help from them then. I circled a few times before I felt ridiculous and stood still. When I took the time to still, I closed my eyes and focused like Harley had taught me. I felt the endless flow of magic in me. I couldn't name it, didn't understand it, but I knew I could use it. I pulled all my love and desire around me, like a cloak. Like a shadow made of intention and need. I thought about where I wanted to be and why it was so important to be there. For Mia and Ny and Gareth. For all of humanity, most likely, because Zeus was a dumbass who wasn't happy with his little corner of power. He wanted an entire world at his feet, worshipping him.

I felt myself slip and shift, like shadow walking only deeper and more ethereal. I wasn't slipping from shadow to shadow, but from realm to realm. Somehow, my will and my magic let me slip from one world to another.

I blinked when I felt arms wrapped tightly around my body. I was back in the arms of Zeus-as-Ny, the same anger and refusal on his face as before. I must have come back to the spot only seconds or less from the time I had left.

Zeus, wearing Ny's face, studied mine, then flinched. He scented me, the motion not smoothly thrilling like it was when Ny was in charge of the body. "No," he hissed out, dropping his arms and shoving me away from him as hard as he could.

I hadn't been expecting that one, so I went flying and landed right on my ass a good five feet from the god in Outer God garb. DD zipped right to me and hovered over me as if studying me. It hesitated a beat, then came close, deciding I was me, even if me was a little changed, and it wanted to be at my side like always. I sent a jolt of appreciation and assurance down the DD tether I felt once again before I wiped my hands of the grime of the tower floor and said, "Rude."

"How is this possible?" he whispered back, taking a defensive stance against me. Seems I didn't need to explain to him what I'd become. He could tell already.

"I had a nice talk with Umar at-Tawil. Gave them the silver key I came by here in the Dreamlands. Presto-change-o, here I am." I spun in my soiled dress and combat boots. "New and improved magic and all."

Zeus didn't reply with words. He chose to zap me with a bolt of lightning. Or, I should say, tried to zap me with a bolt of lightning. My shadow, the magic floating out of me or whatever it was, sang in my ears and I easily side-stepped the intended blow while also wrapping it in my power, making the bolt fizzle out.

I wasn't all-powerful or anything. The split second it took to deflect allowed Zeus to meet me where I stood and punch me right in the gut. I doubled over, the air rushing out of me as pain wracked my body. It was normal, physical pain, and it dulled in comparison to what I had gone through, so I recovered quickly.

"You hit like a human." I sucked in a cloud of shadowy air, letting my new power swell and thump through my body before it shot out of me in rolling waves. I laughed at the god now shaking in front of me.

In answer to my sick burn, he met my power with his own, shoving electricity into my shadows. Enough volts to fry my insides, I assumed, if I were human. The magic took the damage, rode the power, and poured it back out in a billowing cloud of shadow Zeus soon got lost in. I couldn't see him anymore, but I felt him fall away.

Ny's own darkness, the darkness of space, started to pulse weakly in answer to my building power. I needed something else, something to give me space and time to think. I couldn't get Zeus out of Ny by beating him up. I needed something else.

My magic called out for things, things it knew it needed even if I didn't realize what it wanted, and I plunged my hands out of my wavering shadow, out into some other place or space, and clamped them onto two rounded handles. I pulled back with a real, solid, non-DD-composed spear in one hand and a real, solid torch in the other. Seemed my mind had conjured those things before because they were real, and I had the real deal now.

I waved the spear, and the sizzling of magic electricity around Zeus-as-Ny fizzled out, which earned an angry growl from Zeus.

When he eyed the things in my hand, he blanched and scrambled backward. He tried to blast me with more of his power, but my shadows pulled it in and rebounded it, making him freeze, just like I'd seen Ny frozen by his own magic before. I kept my distance, because who knew how long it would last or what it even did. I took the time to look for Gareth, to make sure he was fine.

He and Wilbur were battling it out, but Gareth didn't seem to be in danger, so I pressed on with the god.

I scented the air, like I'd seen Ny do so many times, but I didn't simply smell things. I tasted. I tasted magic and spell, and like with baking, I could now ferret out the components with my tongue. I focused on Zeus-Ny and tasted what had allowed him to take hold of my Prince. I rolled it around my tongue to distinguish the different ingredients of the spell until I found a tether, one string holding the whole composition together.

Without thought, I waved my torch, the flame leaping from my hand to Ny's body and down his throat, where Zeus let out a frantic scream. I directed the flame with my mind, telling it to burn away what was there, what Zeus had used to bind himself to Ny's body. In a flash, Ny dropped to the ground and groaned, flopping from his stomach to his back, his chest heaving deep breaths.

"Sweetling," he croaked, and I knew it was him again.

I dropped my torch and hurried over to scoop him up in my arms, and once again, I really needed to be more mindful when I went to someone's side in battle, because I caught a godly sandaled foot right in the face before I got to Ny.

It knocked me over and to my side, sending me sprawling on the ground, my face a mass of throbbing.

"You stupid bitch," Zeus bit out as he stalked toward me. He was all fury and crackling power, but he'd forgotten I still clung to my spear. I whipped it out, like Gareth had taught me, and caught his feet so he fell to his ass to the ground. Thunder rumbled as I scrambled to my feet again.

"Enough from you, dude. It's over."

He smirked and said, "I think not. Not yet. Not here." His big head nodded toward behind me, where Gareth and Wilbur were, and dammit, I couldn't help but look back just to be sure.

Gareth and Wilbur were somehow fighting in front of a big black hole. Not like a space black hole, but maybe not too far off. It looked like nothingness ripped into the wall, and whatever it was wouldn't be good for my big guy. Gareth was in control though. So much control he was about to toss Wilbur, kicking and cussing, right into the hole.

He did it, Wilbur's furious screams turning to panicked cries as he floated away into the darkness. Gareth was good. Until a zap of Zeus's lightning hit him in the back. He teetered on his feet and stumbled right into the hole. Son of a bitch, it was the Oracle's words. He'd tripped, with the help of Zeus. Lost himself or was about to be lost. I wouldn't let it happen.

I managed to grab Gareth's ankle with a tentacle of the Writhing just in time. He was suspended in the nothingness for a moment before I slowly sucked him back in, bringing him back to the tower and to me.

I knew Zeus was getting up behind me, but I wasn't worried about dealing with him until Gareth lay, shivering and wide-eyed, on the filthy tower floor, safely out of the nothingness in the wall.

By the time I clocked Zeus again, he was staggering toward his own portal in the middle of the room, with the Book of Knowing clutched to his chest and a triumphant smile on his face.

"You did me a favor, Miranda Carter. I'm back in my preferred form, only now I have some special spells I plucked out of Nyarlathotep's mind." He had a limp for some reason, and I hoped the reason hurt. I shot out the Writhing, commanding it to cling to him, stop him. He zapped it with lightning, enough to stop it for the few seconds it took him to step into whatever world he was going to.

"I will find you again, soon, Miranda. And I will rip Hecate's power from you before we are finished."

He disappeared so I couldn't take his ass out, so I screamed in anger and frustration.

"Hecate," Rich whispered, his head bowed and eyes down.

Well, hell. Guess I found some answers to what I was after all, though I had no idea what it meant, and my guys, the ones who might be able to tell me, were each lying on the floor in not-so-great shape.

"Whatever," I muttered, brushing the idea aside. Ny and Gareth were hurt but living and in control of their own skin. Rich seemed fine and had taken care to shield Mia. I let out a breath I hadn't known I was holding—a breath I'd probably left locked in my chest since Wilbur had kidnapped my sister—and crumpled to the floor myself, needing just a tiny breather after all the mess.

Twenty Three

I FELT NY BESIDE me. He hadn't bothered to get up off the floor yet. Instead, he scooched in next to me, looking pretty damn rough. I'm sure I looked no better. I knew Gareth looked no better because I could see his ghost-white face from here. And, oddly, a shock of black streaking his blond hair.

"Sweetling. Are you well?"

"Just peachy." My voice croaked, so strained I was sure not a soul believed the words. "You good? Whole?"

I heard Ny's sigh, felt his hand creep up to clench my own at my side, then still, jolting as if struck. He came up on an elbow to hover over my face. "What is this?" His free hand hovered over my body, as if stroking the shadows I was throwing off. Those shadows shivered in his wake, making me shiver in kind.

"Oh, the power? Got it from your bro's guard at the silver gate. Which was the black stone cave place I'd been dreaming of, by the way."

"She holds the power of Hecate," Rich growled from his position holding my sister. His lip was curled in a half snarl he directed at Ny, which was super weird because they were supposedly friends. Ny quirked an eyebrow his way, and Rich's hackles went down just a little.

"Things are beginning to come together. However, I cannot imagine how it's possible."

"Do I even want to know?"

"Hecate was a god. Not only a god, a titan. One of the old gods before gods," Gareth whispered from across the room. I turned my head toward him and my cheek scraped against the rocky grime of the stone floor. Figuring I was gross enough, I dragged myself up to sitting before I asked, "Are you okay, Gareth?"

"Not quite," he answered honestly, "but I will be. Give me a moment, Randy."

I looked at Ny. "Can you get up?"

He heaved himself off the ground, his body lacking its normal feline grace. "I will need to heal from what Zeus did to this form while he was inside it, as he was not considerate with how he rode my power." He flexed muscles, twisted and turned, and surveyed his human body before saying, "I will heal quickly, and am well enough for whatever you may require, Randy."

He pulled me up off the floor with ease as I said, "Not me. Gareth."

Ny went to him, kneeling beside my big guy, and fingered the dark lock of hair at his right temple. "I am sorry, friend, for what you experienced."

"Which was?" I asked.

"Nothing."

"But you just said…"

"No, Randy. You misunderstand. He experienced nothing, as in the actual cessation of any sensation. The blank dark."

Not good then.

"Gareth?"

He groaned as he sat up. "I promise, Randy. I will be well. I'll need some time, maybe some therapy, but I'll be okay."

Ny laid a hand on Gareth's shoulder and said, "I know the feeling. If you wish to discuss it, I am available."

They gave each other bro-ish head nods, and I shouldered my way between them to hug them both. Ny's magic sang with mine, a new harmony more robust and fuller than my original thrum but hitting the same notes. Gareth's calm was almost gone. It squeezed my gut, thinking he'd maybe lost it for good. Yet I felt a smidge of it somewhere in him, and the new bits of me with a taste for magic told me he would recover.

I moved to Mia, who was looking better and better by the minute. Rich's power slammed into me, but not because he'd tried. I was more attuned to magic, and something of the ghoul in him was kin to what was flowing through me.

He noticed my hesitation and cast his eyes down. "It's the moon connection," he grumbled, shuffling back to get out of my way as if I'd hurt him. As if he needed to be below me, appear lesser than me.

"Um, Rich. This is weird, and I don't understand it, but I know Mia's happy to have you near, and from what Ny and the other ghouls said, you likely saved my little sis from a lot of shit. You don't need to divert your eyes or bow or whatever. You and me? We're good."

He visibly swallowed, his bright-blue eyes flashing in the dim light, and for the first time, I noticed the long line of his rugged face, his swimmer's body full of lean muscles, and his thick, neatly trimmed brown hair, and I thought maybe Mia had noticed those things too, what with the way she stayed touching him the whole time.

"As you wish," he answered. It was too subservient. I didn't like it, but there was not much I could do about it in the moment. I needed to see to Mia and figure out how to get her back to the human realm ASAP.

"Mia? How about you? You good?"

"Just peachy," she said, mimicking me, and I gave her a harsh laugh.

"How's, uh, the book and stuff?"

"Zeus didn't get it." She tapped the side of her rather greasy black hair. "Still fully integrated into my matrix."

Didn't know what to do with that info, or if it was good or bad, but at least Zeus didn't have copies of both books.

"But he got some of the spells?"

"Yes. I tried, Randy. I did. I held out for a long time. Rich helped, but..." She drifted off, a haunted look in her eye and a frown on her face.

"Hey. Hey. It's okay. You did great. You're here and healthy. That's all that matters."

She burrowed into Rich's chest, and he stroked her back, a comforting gesture I was happy to see her accept. Hopefully, she'd take comfort from me again soon.

"Right. So..." I pushed up to standing and dusted bits of who-knows-what off my dress. "We need to get out of here, quick. Then, we have to figure out where Zeus is and how we can stop him."

"First," Ny said, close to my right side. I felt his power stretch out, traveling down into the Palace proper, and a sizzle on my senses told me a second before Gupan and Ugar materialized in room.

"What has happened here?" the talking one said, anger making his voice boom.

"Zeus has defied me and attempted to overthrow my rule. He will be punished, as will those who encouraged his ego. You are to immediately detain Hera, Odin, and Discordia as accomplices to his revolt."

The silent one had murder in his expression, but he disappeared in a blink to do Ny's biding.

"What do you wish to add, Gupan?" Ny asked, finally letting me know the chatty one was Gupan and the mostly quiet one was Ugar.

Gupan looked me up and down before answering. "Ugar will confine the three to cells, as requested. You may interrogate them at your leisure. As for you, Randy Carter. You may return any time you wish. A throne awaits."

"What?" I was more than a little disbelieving.

Ny waved Gupan on and said, "We will discuss more soon enough. For now, simply do as I command."

The god bowed to Ny, then me and blinked out.

"What the hell, Ny?" I asked.

"As Gareth said, you have the power of a god now, Randy. Why, I do not know. All of what you were able to do previously mimicked Hecate's powers, so I assume all of it was locked away inside. You unlocked all of it with the silver key."

"You're saying I'm a god?"

"At least as close to it as a human can achieve." He rubbed a hand on his forehead, either in pain or worry.

"Who was Hecate?"

"A friend. One of the only friends I had in this court. She was killed eons ago."

"How do you kill a god?"

"We'll need to figure it out," Gareth said, stepping up to our little huddle. I swallowed hard. He was right. We'd need to find out for several reasons, involving who and what I was and what we'd need to do in the future.

"Okay. Whatever. No time to worry about that can of worms this second. We need to get out of here, get Mia back and safe, update Merry and Harley. Then we can figure out what I became, why, and how we can track down Zeus."

"I believe we will not need to find him. He will find us." Ny said this as he looked at Mia and Rich with a frown on his face. Just great. She still wasn't safe.

Rich growled in response to Ny's unspoken words and hugged my sister tighter. "I'm coming to the human realm with you, to help guard Mia."

I was more than cool with it. I wanted Mia to have all the guards she could if Zeus was still out to get her and the book. We still needed to get back before more could be figured out. "How are we doing this? Riding shadows to a spot where we can reach the in-between, then hike to the graveyard?"

Ny waved a hand over my shadowy form. "No need to ride shadows. You and I can open a path."

"So certain?"

"I know the magic I feel from you. It can be done."

"Let's get to it then."

Ny took my hand, raised our joined fists in front of us, and sent magic out. Mine followed in kind, my shadow and his space swirling together to form a hole in the tower wall leading to the strange forest with neon mushrooms and zoogs scurrying around where we entered the Dreamlands. The in-between.

"Good, good," I said. "We have to keep hold like last time?"

He squeezed my hand and said, "It's always best."

It was not a hardship to hold Ny's strong, magic-tingling hand, so I waved Mia forward.

"Hold on tight to me and hold on tight to Rich. Don't let go of either of us. We'll be home real quick."

Gareth moved around to grab Ny's other hand without a word, and we all stepped as a unit into the in-between. It was a short walk from where we'd entered to the willow and the graveyard. Union Cemetery was bathed in bright yellow sunlight, filled to bursting with shades I could now see without even having to think about it.

I blinked in the sunlight. The ghosts or shades or whatever looked more solid and real to me, and every shadow stood out, longer and darker than I remembered shadows ever being when they weren't DD or the Writhing. Magic and earth, shades and shadows rushed over my senses, telling me I was home, even if I weren't exactly the same at home anymore.

DD was hovering close, had been for a while, waiting for whatever I might need. "Could you please get Harley? Let her know we need both her and Merry driving."

DD did its nodding thing, then disappeared. I knew Merry and Harley would be here as soon as they could, no questions asked.

We were out of the Dreamlands, Mia was safe for now, and I had a riot of power ponding in my body. I wobbled a step, then plopped my butt onto the soft grass, feeling woozy as the adrenaline started to leech from me.

"Randy," Mia called, coming to kneel by me.

"Just need a minute, sis. I'm all good. Promise."

Well, maybe not all good. I'd get there now because Mia wasn't a prisoner, and I apparently had the magical powers of a god. Power enough to do what needed to be done to help the people I loved.

"I love you, Mia," I said.

She hugged me tight, tears clogging her voice when she said, "I love you so much."

I looked up at Ny and Gareth, no longer afraid of what might happen. Not in this way.

"I love you two too, you know. Both of you. So I'm real glad you're okay and here with me now."

Gareth shuddered out a breath and gave me a hard stare. Ny smiled his feline smile. "I knew you'd say it, sweetling. Didn't realize it would be while you were so dirty."

"That's not a great reply, Prince," I groused.

Ny scooped me up off the ground with an easy grace. "I love you above all things past and present in this universe."

Gareth crowded me in, finally finding his voice. "I love you too, Randy. So much it hurts sometimes."

It was the way of it, right? Sometimes love hurt, but it also felt too good to give up. "Better answers," I said, teasing.

Ny set me on my feet so he could give me a long, slow kiss, which caused my magic blood to pump a staccato rhythm. Gareth's diminished calm brushed against my shadow, and I felt better about him. He reached out, took my mouth from Ny, and gave me his own deep kiss. My guys were here with me, had been with me every step of the way, and were now firmly rooted inside me. No digging them out or running away. They were there to stay.

I saw Mia and Rich having their own moment together and left them to it. DD zipped back, having completed its mission. I leaned between Gareth and Ny and waited for the rest of our ragtag team to get here so we could start dealing with the aftermath of what had happened here and what had gone down in the Dreamlands.

Twenty Four

A FEW DAYS AFTER my return from the Dreamlands, I stood crying in the dying light of the afternoon as Deb's casket was lowered into the ground. Merry was on one side, her arm around me, squeezing me tight. Harley stood beside her, offering her silent but strong support to us both. Gareth and Ny stood at my back, both gentlemanly and courteous to everyone, ready to jump in to soothe or comfort if I needed them. They'd always be at my back. I'd waved to the Warm Regards employees I'd seen, including Nate, who'd hovered around the edges of the crowd, not coming in too close. I didn't blame him for maintaining distance, but I did need to talk with him sometime soon.

I kind of wanted distance from the tragedy of it all right then too, but I couldn't let myself have it. I was close, though not up with the family, but it was more from a sense of bearing witness to the horrible thing I'd allowed to happen in my place, on my watch. No one outside my little magic circle knew that, of course, because a very different turn of events had been given to the authorities and Deb's family.

Apparently, the story Ny had told the cops—and Merry had backed up through all her calls and planning—was that a gas line beside my building had had a mini explosion. Helpful or not, Ny had sent shadows to cause havoc down there and rip a small hole in my outer wall. How anyone would think it possible and not cause much more damage than a gash in one brick bakery, I didn't know. I didn't want to know. It was what it was. I wasn't blamed for Deb's death by her family or the cops, though the blame laid heavy in my chest, a lead weight I'd carry for a real long time. Possibly my whole life.

All I could do now was honor her as best I could. And avenge her, even if vengeance was more important to the living than the dead. Deb sure as hell wasn't caring about it right then, not as I stood crying and seething in the small crowd gathered by her headstone, watching her mom and dad weep as they tossed flowers into her grave.

I glanced over at Harley. The hard, grim line of her mouth told me she was as angry as I was about this, was as ready as I was to get the vengeance we needed. Starry Wisdom was gone, but Harley knew Zeus had orchestrated all of it, from the original deaths that had drawn her into her hunt to this death, the murder of a woman her girlfriend cared about. She'd be down for whatever we needed to do, and we needed something to do, damnit. Now Mia was back, the anger raged over the worry, and all I knew was Zeus had to be stopped, and he had to pay for what he'd done.

I felt Gareth's warm, firm hand on my shoulder and a second later felt the intentional zig of Ny's power skitter down my spine, all reminders of what came before and what we needed to do next. We hadn't had a lot of opportunities to discuss what all had gone down in the Dreamlands, but we would. We'd talk and plan and fight, all together. It was our way now, and I knew it deep in my soul.

The other part I knew, deep in my soul and in the blood pumping through my veins, was I was magic and shadow, godly power made flesh, with no real rhyme or reason to it I could pinpoint yet. I was the bearer of Hecate's lost power. I was feared by gods and by ghouls, and I was definitely not fully human now, if I was ever human at all. More research was needed, more time to learn and train and grow, but I didn't know if I had enough time, or if I deserved to take the time if I had it.

Deb lay in the ground at my feet because she'd stepped into my world, and there were so many people beyond her who'd paid for being close to me. Mia, for sure. Merry had her own connection to me and my magic now, and who knows what it meant, seeing as I was goddess-esque or something and she had a direct line to my mind. Harley and Gareth had already been in the occult world, searching for something, but they hadn't bargained for a fight with a god. I had to use my power to get everyone free and clear, make sure Zeus was neutralized before I even began to think about myself.

Dusk spread quickly, and despite the clear sky, I heard thunder rumble in the distance. If thunder was there, lightning would follow. Zeus would cause whatever destruction and ruin he could to wrest back the power over people he thought was his due. My hand clenched and DD shook at my side. He'd try, but I was god-like now too, and he'd get every bit of my shadow and magic I could throw at him. I'd force it down his throat and, somehow, figure out how I could kill a god.

Please take a moment to rate Shadow in the Dreamlands on Amazon. Every rating/review helps!

If you liked what you read and want more, consider preordering Book 4, Shadow of the Other Gods, on Amazon right now.

Stay up-to-date with all things Sonya Lawson at sony alawson.com.

Want More?

Interested in what Nyarlathotep was up to before he walked into Warm Regards? Join my newsletter and get a (very steamy) prequel story featuring the Prince of the Dreamlands. Visit BookFunnel to download the free story.

There's also a free prequel novella all about Randy, Merry, and Mia you can get with a newsletter sign-up. Download *Shadow in the Storm* today!

Don't forget to preorder Book 4, *Shadow of the Other Gods*, on Amazon now. It will drop October 13th, 2023.

Want to read other books by Sonya Lawson? Check out more of her book pages below:

The Comus Duology

In Dreams of Dragons

Acknowledgements

Novel Nurse Editing has been with me for over a year at this point, giving indispensable advice all along the way. They've now helped me perfect four books, and I look forward to their help on many more.

100 Covers again did this amazing cover and I have nothing but praise for their dedication and talent for making Randy come to life in various ways.

The MBs, a fabulous group of writing folks I thankfully call friends, help me daily. They give encouragement and guidance. I'm forever grateful for all they do for me.

My husband, my family, and my friends are all love and encouragement, even if it's a bit gruff and real at times. My life is what it is – beautiful and amazing and full of stories – because they let me be me and love me for me. Thanks for continuing to be great.

This third book in The Chronicles of Randy Carter is the last book to strictly follow the plot points of a specific Lovecraft story. Book 4 is much more of a mishmash, so you can look forward to that soon. For this one, "The Dream-Quest of Unknown Kadath" was

my map. It's a surreal, ridiculous, and often infuriating story with moments of truly specular weird horror
looped into it. I hope I turned it on its head to make
it more inclusive and thoughtful while keeping those
Lovecraftian weird vibes in place.

About the Author

Sonya Lawson is a recovering academic currently writing steamy modern fantasy with maybe a few too many literary references. Her stories may differ, but they all have at least one common characteristic — sassy, intelligent women trying to do the best they can in whatever world they inhabit.

While she remains a rural Kentuckian at heart, she's spent a lot of time in the Midwest and currently lives in the Pacific Northwest. She fills her days with writing, editing, reading, walking through old forests, and watching sitcoms or horror films with her husband. Two rowdy cats terrorize her house regularly, but she loves it.

You can find more information about past books, current projects, and upcoming releases at www.sonyalawson.com.

Don't forget to follow her on all her socials to stay connected. Find her on TikTok, Instagram, and Facebook using her username @sonyalawsonwrites.